KILLER ON THE LOOSE

For $1,000 Harvey Munson undertook to deliver $50,000 to Garfield Creek City Bank. However, the thief who waylaid him didn't know he was tangling with a wild cat and died as a result. Then, back in his hometown of Turlock, Harvey had another shock for Sheriff Grant Watson, his surrogate father, was ambushed and murdered. On top of that, Harvey was accused of murder and jailed pending trial. Soon guns roared and blood flowed with an outcome that was by no means certain.

KILLER ON THE LOOSE

by

Elliot Long

Dales Large Print Books
Long Preston, North Yorkshire,
BD23 4ND, England.

British Library Cataloguing in Publication Data.

Long, Elliot
    Killer on the loose.

    A catalogue record of this book is
    available from the British Library

    ISBN   978-1-84262-614-6 pbk

First published in Great Britain 2007 by Robert Hale Limited

Copyright © Elliot Long 2007

Cover illustration © Gordon Crabb by arrangement with
Alison Eldred

Published in Large Print 2008 by arrangement with
Robert Hale Ltd.

Dales Large Print is an imprint of Library Magna Books Ltd.

Printed and bound in Great Britain by
T.J. (International) Ltd., Cornwall, PL28 8RW

CHAPTER ONE

Made short tempered by the earliness of the day and loss of sleep, hired mankiller Ramos Tomás Blazer walked in through the office door and sat down in the hard-back chair. He gazed across the spur-scarred oak desk at the man he knew as El Lobo.

The Wolf, at this moment, was diligently writing and Ramos thought it was amazing how things changed. Three years ago El Lobo was the greatly feared gringo leader of thirty *bandidos* and *¡caramba!* Didn't they live well under his leadership? Indeed, the booty gained from El Lobo's criminal activities in Mexico and across the Rio Grande was legendary. The reward of $5000 for his capture, dead or alive, placed there by the Texas Rangers and the Mexican authorities, was still effective – until firm proof of his death was forthcoming and double-checked. Not that he, Ramos Tomás Blazer, would think of taking advantage of such tempting remuneration for the feelings of loyalty he held for El Lobo were still true and firm.

But why did El Lobo leave them?

Pensively, Ramos rubbed his chin. It could only be what happened those three years ago in Cañon Sorpresa, deep in the high sierras, that caused the irrevocable change; the day the Rurales finally trapped the whole gang as they returned to their stronghold after two successful bank robberies.

What a blood bath it was!

However, a few of the gang escaped, including Ramos Tomás Blazer. El Lobo was last seen riding up the canyon with three Rurales on his back-trail.

Some of the surviving compadres suggested they go to El Lobo's aid, but why? Were they not in enough trouble themselves? El Lobo could take care of himself. He was not a child. What was needed at that moment, most decided, was for every man to make his own escape.

In any case, remembered Ramos, El Zorro, The Fox, went after the Rurales chasing El Lobo. El Zorro was the slick one. He would think of something. He would help El Lobo. And the proof soon came that he did.

Two weeks later the carcases of the pursuing Rurales were found. The last to be discovered, it was reported by search parties, was unfortunate enough to be captured by El Lobo and El Zorro. It was said the Rurale's injuries were worse than any Apache could inflict. However, decided Ramos, it was gratifying to know what happened to their compadres in Cañon Sorpresa had been suitably avenged.

But then nothing from El Lobo: it was as though the ground just swallowed him up. Now this request out of the blue: once more The Wolf required the services of his right-hand man – the *pistolero*, Ramos Tomás Blazer. But this time, there were certain conditions to be met. Foremost of them, El Lobo insisted, Ramos must tell none of his present lawless compadres of this lucrative contract he was being offered by his one-time leader. And above all, he must come to this gringo town of Turlock alone.

Ramos gazed across the desk at El Lobo. The Wolf was now finished with his papers and was twirling the pen in his hand and staring at him. A glance through the small window behind El Lobo told Ramos the dawn sun was now rising gloriously and that the cold drapes of pre-dawn mists spreading wispy tendrils across the cold desolate streets were now dispersing.

El Lobo said, 'I said four thirty. It's gone

five o'clock.'

Ramos smiled and spread his arms. 'You know I am a man of the night, *patrón*. Such habits are not easily broken.'

El Lobo scowled. 'Yeah, and that was why you didn't get the full story last night – in case you ran your mouth off to some damn whore.'

Ramos went taut for a moment. Was it suggested he could not keep a secret? That was an unwarranted insult, but Ramos forgave it. There were good rewards to be earned. And things had not been easy of late. Above all, he must be careful. Discretion was needed now he was back in the employ of El Lobo.

The Wolf was now fiddling impatiently with the papers on his desk. 'Now, where did we get to last night?'

'You explained to me how I was to kill this gringo *vaquero*, Harvey Munson, in the High Tip Mountains, but that was all,' Ramos said. 'You added the rest of the plan you would leave until now: that you didn't have the time.' Ramos grinned roguishly and preened his thick black moustache. 'Perhaps you had another engagement, uh, *patrón?*' he suggested. 'A certain *señorita*, maybe?'

El Lobo's glare was ice cold. 'Keep your

8

damned filthy greaser opinions to yourself, all right?'

Again Ramos tightened. Again he subdued his resentment, but it was hard. He shrugged. 'If you insist.'

El Lobo twirled the pen. 'Now, let's get down to business, because you've got a deal of riding to do to get this job done on time.'

Ramos smiled. 'I am waiting, *patrón*.'

El Lobo leaned forward and stabbed out a fat finger. 'You kill Munson in the High Tips, got it? Then you bring the saddle-bags he's carrying back to this office – unopened.' El Lobo's hard gaze reached across the desk. '*Unopened*, understand? And when you get back to this office you check to see I'm alone before you enter. It won't look good you being seen in here talking to me.'

Ramos spread his arms. '*Patrón*, I am not known this side of the border and is it likely you will have company in the middle of the night?'

El Lobo scowled across the desk. 'Just do it, right?'

'Of course,' Ramos said.

But, Ramos thought, what is in those saddle-bags, gold? Or even better, gringo dollars? It was a huge possibility, mused Ramos, if El Lobo was involved. A leopard

9

does not change his spots; he is stuck with them. Even better, if he were to relieve El Lobo of that burden the world would be at Ramos Tomás Blazer's feet. But that would not be easy. El Lobo was his *patrón*. Any ideas he might profit from this assignment – apart from the generous remuneration he was already receiving for doing the job – was unthinkable. And on top of that, was he not the most trusted as well as the most feared *pistolero* in all Mexico? Was it not well known that when Ramos Tomás Blazer was asked to fulfil a contract he did it efficiently and with scrupulous honesty? Pah! This gringo *vaquero*, Harvey Munson – he was already dead! And Ramos Tomás Blazer's honour would remain intact as always.

Ramos smiled benignly. *Si*, the hard times were over. Once more he was in the service of his *patron*. It felt good.

'What's so funny?' El Lobo said.

Ramos spread arms. 'Why, nothing, *patron*? I was just thinking how fortunate I am that–'

'Thinking, uh?' El Lobo growled. 'Well, *amigo*, you're not paid to think; you're paid to act. You got that?'

'*Si*, but–'

'But nothing, right?'

The Wolf leaned back in his swivel chair

and twirled the pen between his fingers. 'Now, did you get a good look at Munson?'

'Of course,' said Ramos.

El Lobo said, 'Good, because I don't want any mistakes. Like killing the wrong man and bringing in the wrong bags.'

Ramos frowned. He was now a trifle confused. This was not the old El Lobo. 'Why do you continue to insult me, *patron?*' he said. 'Two days I watched this *hombre*. I know him better than I knew my mother, may the saints give her peace. What is this weevil eating at your belly, uh? It is not like you. And you know when I am asked to do a job it will be done right.'

El Lobo scowled. 'I don't want any foul-ups.'

Ramos now found a coolness beginning to permeate through him, and resentment. He stared across the desk. '*Patrón*, if you think my services are not of the highest quality, why bring me here? Why not do the job yourself? It is not as though you are the amateur.'

El Lobo cut air with a beefy hand. 'Because I've got other fish to fry,' he said. 'Now get out of here, I've got work to do.'

But Ramos was shocked. It was as if El Lobo was dismissing some *campesino*, some peasant. Deep hurt filled the *pistolero*. There

11

was a time when El Lobo showed him great respect. If he was to remain a man he could not allow this latest insult to go by un-answered.

'I will have your apology now, *patrón*, or the deal is off,' he said.

El Lobo's gaze came up and his brows came together to form a fleshy overhang above his eyes.

'Did you say apologize?'

'*Sí.*'

For a moment El Lobo stared at Ramos, as if in disbelief. The *pistolero* could almost see the old evil rekindling itself in his *patrón*'s eyes.

As a precaution Ramos moved his hand nearer to his Remington cap-and-ball pistol in the holster at his right thigh. However, he was reasonably certain El Lobo would not react violently. He knew The Wolf wanted this job done so badly he would take nearly any indignity to see it through. But it was clear El Lobo was trembling in suppressed rage – so much so he broke the pen in his ham-like hand. Nevertheless, he said, as if spitting out bitter gall, 'OK. I'm *sorry*. Will that do?'

The metallic edge to El Lobo's voice sug-gested he was anything but regretful, however Ramos accepted it as an apology of sorts and returned his mind – but this time with new anticipation – to the saddle-bags the gringo *vaquero*, Harvey Munson, would be carrying through the mountains. Yes, Ramos decided, it was time he adjusted his loyalties for it was clear he no longer had the respect of his *patrón*. And there was another thing to be considered: Ramos Tomás Blazer was not getting any younger – a fact that could not be ignored. And he was now realistic enough to believe the day was fast coming when even he, the greatest of *pistoleros*, would be that microsecond too slow and...

Ay, yi, yi!

Ramos closed his mind. He would not think upon such things. Instead he would think of his beloved Juanita, the children that already graced his *casa* and the boys and girls he fully intended to sire in the future. All that would need paying for. And if there was a lot of dollars or gold in those saddlebags the gringo *vaquero* would be carrying – and taking into account the loss of respect that was now very apparent between himself and El Lobo – the way was now clear to take advantage of the situation.

But again he closed his mind. Such a thing

was unthinkable. *¡Caramba!* El Lobo was his *patrón*. Loyalty to that fact ran deep. It was engrained in the society he grew up in. El Patrón was inviolate. Yes, he would try once more to get on more amicable terms with his *jefe*.

'Do you remember Juanita, *patrón?*' he said. 'How beautiful she is? How she is always hungry for my love?'

Deadpan, El Lobo stared at him.

'What about her, Goddamn it?'

Despite the impatience in El Lobo's voice Ramos smiled broadly and spread his arms. 'I would only like to tell you nothing has changed between us,' he said. 'Juanita remains a jewel amongst jewels – the brightest star in the firmament of ugliness that is all around us.'

El Lobo's lips curled into a sneer. 'Are you trying to tell me you are still running around with that whore, you dumb bastard? Jesus, Ramos, for a handful of pesos she'd spread her legs for anyone – what I recall.'

Ramos stared. Hatred consumed him, like a many-headed Hydra. *Patrón* or no, such an insult to the name of his wife and thus to her family, and his, was the final affront. He said, with slight regret, 'Always you make the joke, uh, *patrón?*' Stiffly, he rose from his

14

chair and crossed to the stout, little-used rear door of the office. At it he turned. 'Until tonight, my friend.'

El Lobo waved an irritable arm and growled, 'Get out of here, will you?'

Ramos opened the door and stepped down into the weeds and trash in the alley beyond. He closed the door quietly behind him. Now standing in the diamond-sharp shadows of the dawn, the chill of this high-country morning dug deeply into him. He hunched his back against its rawness and set his flat-topped *torero* hat at an angle and put a thin stogie into his mouth. He chewed on it thoughtfully before lighting it, and then he drew on it and inhaled.

Trickling smoke out of his nostrils he looked towards the hitch rack at the end of this narrow backstreet. Tethered there, his roan was pawing impatiently at the mixture of horse dung and yellow dust beneath its iron-shod hoofs. That was another thing he thought: this order to tether the gelding there in case tying it up out front connected El Lobo to Ramos Tomás Blazer.

A curse on the son of a pig!

Ramos trickled more tobacco smoke out of his nostrils. If there was plenty of *dinero* in those saddlebags the gringo would be carrying, and he was to steal it... El Lobo must die also. Because, if he did not kill him El Lobo would surely hunt him down like he was some rabid dog and butcher him without mercy, as he had done the Rurales those three years ago in the high sierras.

Ramos caressed the haft of the Spanish stiletto in the belt sheath across the small of his back. His killing instincts warmed up. Such a blade, skilfully inserted – and he was very good at such things – into the right parts of living flesh, produced no noise other than the sigh of a quick death.

Ramos's mind grew expansive. After stealing El Lobo's plunder and killing him he now envisaged the huge hacienda he would build in Old Mexico, envisaged the brisk trade in rustled Texas beef and further remuneration from successful bank raids and stage hold-ups across the border and elsewhere. On top of that, the local *alcalde* and Rurales bought and paid for and no longer a worry.

Ramos smiled. The horizons were un-limited. And with Juanita by his side and their many *muchachos* running wild over their vast acres, his cup of life would indeed be brimming over.

No longer feeling the cold, Ramos walked

briskly to his tethered mount. He untied the reins and swung up into the ornate Mexican saddle. He put the horse into a brisk canter and within seconds he was out of the shadows and into the dawn sunlight flooding across the open chaparral levels beyond Turlock's town limits. Now the path he was to ride was clear he ticked off his immediate requirements in his mind. He would kill this gringo *vaquero*, Harvey Munson, then return to Turlock and kill the *patrón* he once revered, almost as a god. After that, he would return to El Paso to pick up Juanita and the children and move over the border into Old Mexico and happiness. But there was one other thing. El Zorro ... would he intervene? It was well known he and El Lobo were like brothers, never parted. El Zorro was also a very dangerous man. If he chose to avenge El Lobo's death, Ramos Tomás Blazer would have to kill El Zorro, too, like the vermin he was named after. But death, was it not all part of living?

Ramos smiled once more as he stared at the High Tip range thirty-five miles ahead. They were giant snow-capped peaks erupting out of the early morning mists into the blue vault of the early day.

He fondled his horse's ears. 'Amigo,' he

said, 'I have got the feeling there is going to be one very dead gringo in those hills pretty soon and, tonight, one very dead *patrón* here in town. And because of that I am going to be made a very rich man.'

Ramos's laugh was harsh on the morning air. So grating was it that it caused the birds to flutter up and shriek warnings into the pristine sky. It also sent the lizards basking on the rocks in the new day's sunshine scurrying for cover.

CHAPTER TWO

It was now an hour before noon. The old town of Turlock was sizzling under the hot sun. The searing heat was driving most people inside for an early siesta, or a couple of cool beers in any one of the three shady *cantinas* this end of the town boasted. However, the heat didn't appear to be affecting ageing Grant Watson, long-serving sheriff of this town. He was wide-awake, his blue stare keen. He was standing on the boardwalk outside the adobe law office and the recently built brick jail attached to its rear.

Grant appeared to be completely impervious to the sun's blistering torment.

A grin wrinkled his brown, leathery face. He touched the brim of his sweat-stained, once white, ten-gallon Stetson hat in salute as he gazed at Harvey Munson, his adopted son. The boy was now foreman of the Crossed R ranch – the spread that covered a sizable piece of the Culibar Hills, twenty miles to the south in this huge Sontan Basin. Harvey was sitting tall atop his big steel-grey gelding before the law office four-horse tie-rail. The burro behind him on the lead rope was looking decidedly miserable in the heat. Grant Watson knew the beast was carrying trail victuals plus the fifty-thousand dollars in large denomination bills, to be delivered to Garford Creek's City Bank.

Harvey was grinning teasingly down at him.

'You're trusting me with an awful lot of *dinero*, Pa,' he said. 'What's to say I won't just keep riding north, uh?'

The lawman's returned smile was easy. 'I know you better than that. I raised you good. I know you wouldn't even think about such things, apart from using it to tease me. So get your ass along that trail, boy, and have a good trip now.'

19

Harvey raised brows. 'All being well, I guess.'

Sheriff Grant Watson gave out with a disparaging snort before he dropped the timbre of his voice and looked furtively round before he whispered, 'All being well nothing! There isn't a thing can go wrong. I keep telling you, you'll be back before you know it and will be a thousand dollars the richer for your trouble. That's got to be good pay in any man's language. Damn it, boy, I set the whole thing up. D'you think I'd put you in the way of any danger?'

Harvey said, 'Well, it ain't likely.'

'Damned right it isn't,' said the sheriff. 'As I explained, only three people know about the fifty thousand you're carrying – me, you and one other whose money it is but wants his name kept out of it. Dammit, son, none of us three are likely to talk openly about the shipment, are we?'

'Wouldn't make a lot of sense,' said Harvey. 'But it's an awful lot of money, Pa.' Still in a teasing mood he added, 'Is it straight?'

Grant Watson glared fiercely and shuffled irritably. 'I'll pretend I didn't hear that, boy.' Then he narrowed his eyelids. 'But, since you brought it up – don't take anything for granted.'

'You figure somebody else might get to know?'

The lawman said, 'It's a possibility and you should be aware of it.'

The warning sobered Harvey a little. No doubt about it, there were plenty of hard-cases prowling this territory now gold had been discovered in the Snake Back country to the northwest. Indeed, there were men who would give their eyeteeth to get their hands on the kind of money he was carrying. And there was another thing that added credence to his present thinking.

Almost from the moment he arrived in town two days ago from the Crossed R he got this feeling he was being watched, followed. It was so bad it became like an itch he couldn't scratch, a cold crawly sensation up his backbone. Nevertheless, every time he turned to try and locate the source of his unease all he encountered were milling crowds of miners, speculators, and gamblers, the general run of quick-eyed hardcases – indeed, the whole restless tide of humanity that was now flooding this once peaceful cow-town of Turlock. Silently, he cursed his nervousness. It seemed like he was sensing danger at every turn. It wasn't like him. But fifty-thousand dollars in high denomination bills was a lot of *dinero* to be carrying and he was right to be cautious. At one time he was so concerned he played with the idea of voicing his suspicions about being tailed to his pa, but, dammit, he was a big boy now. He could deal with his own problems.

He touched the wide brim of his hat.

'Well, I'll see you in five days, old timer.'

Sheriff Watson nodded and said, 'Sure you will, and I'll be looking out for you. I'll have a beer set up on Coley's Bar to celebrate your return.'

Harvey smiled and relaxed. 'Sounds good.'

He gazed fondly at the ageing lawman. In all ways except being blood kin Grant Watson was his father. And he knew the story behind the adoption. When his real ma and pa died of the cholera eighteen years ago – he was only five at the time – this gruff sheriff of Turlock stepped in and undertook the responsibility of rearing of him. Years later, when he got round to asking the old law dog why he did, he replied, as if he was surprised the question even needed to be asked, 'Because I promised your ma and pa I would, boy. Ain't that enough?'

That reply of years ago sobered Harvey, even now. Yeah, that was enough in Sheriff Grant Watson's book. The man's integrity shone out of him like a beacon. Harvey touched the brim of his hat again.

'I'll be seeing you, Pa.'

'You going to sit there jawing all day?' growled the sheriff.

Smiling, Harvey turned his steel-grey and, trailing the burro on the lead rope behind him, went loping up Turlock's wide, wheel-rutted Main Street. Three minutes later he picked up the stage road to Garford Creek.

Out on the shimmering levels the noon temperature beat down like a sledgehammer. It caused Harvey to hunker down in the saddle. It was vicious heat that prickled a man's eyes, seared his back and sucked moisture out of him like it was being siphoned off. It was heat a man lived with but never got used to, in his experience anyway. Yes, it was suffered, but not patiently, along with the pestering flies.

Ever-watchful Harvey swivelled his gaze and picked out the Snake Back country, fifteen miles to the northwest. Its terracotta-coloured palisades shimmered in the quivering heat. As long back as he could remember, the opinion in the Sontan Basin was the Snake Backs – while being wildly beautiful country – were of little commercial value. Indeed, the early pioneers said it was land too wild and dry and rock-tangled to be used for raising cattle or for tilling soil and was better left to be appreciated for what it was – swell-looking country. And for years it stayed that way. However, a few months ago some crazy old sourdough came whooping into town waving a bagful of placer gold he panned out of one of the many creeks that wriggled their way through the maze of canyons and secret places out there.

That did it.

Soon entrepreneurs, gamblers, prospectors, miners, whores or just plain adventurers began flooding into Sontan Basin. And with such a tremendous influx of humanity, canvas or clapboard dancehalls, saloons and gambling halls, tents for living in and for whoring in, mushroomed overnight. It wasn't long before every vice known to man was offered and there was no shortage of humanity flocking to indulge in them. And as the flow of gold increased and more and more rotgut whiskey was poured, killings became commonplace; mayhem the order of the day.

Harvey tightened his already range-narrowed eyelids. But the gold fever didn't touch him. He was a cowman through and through. From being a boy of twelve, he worked for Slim Pickett out at the Crossed R – one of several ranches situated south, in the green Culibar Hills, so unlike this dry northern end of the eighty miles long, fifty miles wide Sontan Basin.

Rocking in the saddle, Harvey reviewed the past three years of his life; the years since he was appointed foreman at the Crossed R at the age of twenty.

With the job came concessions. One enabled him to run a small herd of his own on the range. On top of that, higher wages and bonuses which helped him to build up a healthy nest-egg. Now the icing on the cake was this thousand dollars he was to receive for delivering the fifty thousand to Garford Creek City Bank. Those wages would finally put him in a position to fulfil his one lifelong ambition – that of owning his own spread. And last year he found the perfect place to locate the ranch house.

He was in the habit, during the quiet times at the Crossed R, of hunting alone in the little-explored heartland of the High Tip Mountains. He happened upon a lush, sheltered valley. It was perfect cattle country, prime for settlement and he wasted no time getting the legal ramifications to acquire it sorted out. Soon after, he pioneered a cattle trail out of the mountains to Garford Creek.

He would have liked to gain access to Turlock, being his hometown, but finding a trail south through the jumbled peaks proved difficult. Garford Creek became the place to get victuals and generally socialize as well as sell his beeves. For Garford Creek was still a cow town, pure and simple, unlike Turlock. Further, last summer the Santa Fe Railway pushed a branch line through the Pearl Mountains, the sierras that towered north-east of Garford Creek. This gave the town a lifeline to the transcontinental lines. And almost overnight sidings and cattle-pens were established a mile outside town and cattle-buying agencies for the big meat-packing companies soon established themselves in that now bustling town.

Happy with the way things worked out, Harvey stared across the sun-blistered levels to the High Tips. He could see it all – the corral, the barns, the ranch house he was going to build. Dammit, he could almost hear his beeves lowing as they grazed the fertile acres of his long, wide valley. And making everything complete, last week, Sarah, Slim Pickett's beautiful dark-haired daughter, agreed to be his wife.

But it wasn't a sudden thing, by God.

From the day he went to work for Slim Pickett at the Crossed R at the age of twelve and met Sarah – who was a year younger than he was – a liking for each other bonded them and it wasn't long before friendship blossomed into love.

However, one thing became recently worrying. Slim Pickett was no longer the man he was. Slim slowly deteriorated after his wife of thirty years, Carmen, tragically died of the fever while visiting her sister in Phoenix. Indeed, Slim began to mooch about the ranch talking to himself, not taking much interest in anything. He would stand for hours at the graveside of his wife, sited on the hill above the long, white adobe ranch house he built there in '67 after he mustered out of the Union Army and came West to seek his fortune. He buried Carmen with the boy they lost during the pneumonia epidemic that hit the Basin during the winter of '84.

Harvey narrowed his eyelids. He went with Slim to Phoenix – drove the buckboard to bring back Carmen's body. It was a harrowing time, particularly digging Carmen's grave and burying her remains. It took Sarah weeks to get over the terrible shock of losing her mother.

Slim slowly came back to doing his books,

but little else. Now he was talking about leaving the ranch to him and Sarah and going to live with relatives in Omaha. Sarah was hurt by the announcement – her pa not wanting her to look after him in his declining years. But, as Slim pointed out, she would have enough on her hands when she and Harvey got married and the children came along. He didn't want to burden her with his infirmities. He explained he would keep control of the ranch but wouldn't take much from the spread's profits, which were healthy anyway – just take enough to live on. And when he was dead and gone the whole outfit would belong to them, lock, stock and barrel. He already had the papers drawn up.

Harvey rubbed his chin. It was a mighty generous offer, but he had plans of his own and the announcement put him in a dilemma. There just wasn't an easy way to tell Slim he wasn't interested in the Crossed R; that this valley he found in the High Tips, the ranch he wanted to build on it and run, was what his heart was set on. And Sarah, as soon as he showed her the valley six months ago, fell in love with its beauty and took his side. They both expressed their regrets, naturally – Slim was dear to their hearts and the Crossed R was a fine ranch. But both he and Sarah shared this burning ambition to build and own their own outfit. Indeed, like true Westerners they wanted to make their own mark on this big land. Some said they were fools, bull-headed and obsessive. Maybe they were right, but he and Sarah didn't see it that way.

And the day came when he needed to tell Slim. Slim Pickett eyed him narrowly, making his disappointment clear. Harvey knew Slim looked upon him as the son he never got to raise, the son he lost all those years ago to the pneumonia. Slim was calm at first. He said, 'Can't I change your mind, boy?'

'I guess not.'

After that it was like the top flew off the soda-pop bottle.

'Dammit, you gone crazy, boy?' Slim roared.

'I want my own place, Slim. Simple as that.'

'God-damned stubborn cuss, always was. You'll have the Crossed R soon as I'm gone. Give it some thought.'

'I have, the answer's still no.'

'You haven't give it no thought at all! If you had you'd snap my hand off! Talk to Sarah, she'll give you the right answer.'

'I have. It's the same as mine.'

'You talked her out of it?'

'Didn't need to.'

Slim stomped away cursing blue lights. However, over a glass of applejack after supper, sitting on the stoop that night, Slim was in a mellower mood.

'When I was your age, son, my pa wanted me to stay on and run the farm. A mighty big farm it was – and hugely profitable I might add – but I said no. Like you, I wanted to make my own mark and when I got out of the army I lit out here to the West and never saw my pa again, though I got nothing against him. Crazy, uh?'

'Not the way I see it,' said Harvey.

'No, boy, I guess it isn't.'

Slim sighed and leaned over. 'Just no getting to you, is there? As for that daughter of mine, she's worse than you!' He offered a work-scarred hand. 'I wish you luck, son, I surely do, because, by God, you're going to need it.'

Harvey faded the recollection and clicked his steel-grey into motion and headed for the High Tips.

He would deliver this money he was carrying, pick up his wages and then set the wheels in motion to build his ranch. It wasn't the most satisfactory of situations. He clung to the hope Slim would change his mind and begin tending to ranch affairs more diligently. But he didn't hold out much hope. The bald truth was, far as he could make out, and Sarah agreed, a part of Slim died with Carmen and the Crossed R held too many memories. Harvey squinted into the strong light of the dry country. It was time to move on, to think of the times ahead. It wasn't going to be easy, he would be the first to admit that. But he, Harvey Munson, was going to make his mark on this big land. What's more, Sarah Pickett, soon to be Munson, was going to help him do it.

He stared at the massive bulks of the High Tip Mountains ahead. Tonight he planned to spend the night playing cards with Grover Ash, the Eagle Bluff waystation owner, then use Indian trails through the mountains to Garford Creek in the hope he could cut half a day off the travelling time.

If word didn't get out about the money, things should work out fine.

He urged the steel-grey into the foothills.

CHAPTER THREE

Ramos Tomás Blazer stared over the vast Sontan Basin. From this vantage point in the foothills of the High Tip Mountains the vast bowl looked beautiful. The vivid colours of sunset were beginning to streak the sky and the sun's yellow-orange orb sat like a huge shimmering ball just above the canyons of the Snake Back country, fifteen miles to his right.

Ramos swivelled his gaze. Harvey Munson was looming larger now, picking his way up the winding trail through the foothills towards him.

Ramos hunched his shoulders against the increasing cold. Already, at these elevations, the air was cooling. But, as El Lobo prophesied earlier, the traffic on this section of the Turlock-Garford Creek road would whittle down to nothing as night drew in. And he was right, thought Ramos. What was more, it looked all set to remain that way until morning. Satisfaction filled Ramos. His ambush was all set up. His horse was tethered out of the way, some two hundred yards back in the willows and aspens that were spreading away from this bubbling creek he was hidden near.

He stared at the point where the trail crossed the lively stream, seventy yards away. He smirked. At this silly distance the killing of the gringo *vaquero*, Harvey Munson, would be like taking candy from a baby.

Soothed by the thought, Ramos caressed the rifle clasped in his sinewy right hand. It was a Winchester, Model 1873, oiled, fully loaded and waiting to be put into action. As he held it he experienced a pleasurable feeling – one of love almost. Yes, he did love the gun. It was his mistress, his power.

He pulled the beautiful weapon into his shoulder and sighted it up. He aimed at the spot he expected Munson to pause at to allow himself and his animals to drink their fill after their long, dry ride across the flats.

Then: *Blam!*

Ramos chuckled quietly as he visualized the bloody end of the gringo. He gazed again at the tall figure heading towards him up the winding trail, which was flanked with house-size boulders.

Señor Harvey Munson. After two days of careful study in town Ramos felt he knew this big gringo *vaquero*. Munson gave the impression he was one mean *hombre*. And though his face was young-looking there was strength in it, a quality that caused concern. And the gringo's eyes ... they were ice-grey, ever alert, moving constantly behind narrowed eyelids. As for his weaponry: a Colt Frontier was cased in a plain, oiled holster nestled on his right thigh. A standard Winchester .44 was stowed in the worn saddle-boot by his right knee.

There was a vibrant energy about the man. Indeed, if he, Ramos, were an Apache, the killing of Munson would surely gain him much power and prestige amongst his people. But he was not an Apache and such primitive ideas bored him. It was the price put on a man's head that gave Ramos Tomás Blazer the incentive to take life. That was his power, his prestige.

Ramos nestled the Winchester into his shoulder and sighted up and waited patiently for Munson to reach the river.

While he bided his time once more the vision of the great wealth he was now convinced was coming his way filled his mind with heady, glamorous thoughts. His beautiful Juanita ... standing in the doorway of the sprawling, gleaming white hacienda he was

34

going to build for her; the vision of their many *muchachos* running free across his land; the Texas beef he rustled grazing his vast acres, all fattening up for sale at an excellent price in Mexico City, or some other place. He did not even need to think about the other lucrative exploits he and his gang would get up to.

Ramos creased his pox-marked face into a grin and revealed his tombstone, tobacco-stained teeth. For sure, it would be just like taking candy from a baby.

CHAPTER FOUR

Again Harvey Munson felt worms of anxiety thread through him as he came up to the edge of the willow-and-aspen lined Shadow Creek. Even though the stream bubbled by with a calm, soothing sound he found its tranquillity did not help his uneasiness one bit. Once more he got this tingling up his backbone, the impression he was being watched. Indeed, the feeling was now so acute it drew his nerves up as tight as fence wire. But the final clincher was: no birds sang. To a country boy, that spoke volumes.

He discreetly scanned his surrounds. Hell, it could be nothing. However, the atmosphere all around suggested it was otherwise. Hardly a leaf rustled or a twig moved. Every fibre in his body was telling him to get the hell out of there and fast.

From his right came the metallic click of what sounded like a gun hammer coming down on a dud cartridge. Then curses in Spanish and the familiar noise of a new load being jacked into the breech of a rifle.

But by the second sound Harvey was already moving. He released the burro to its own devices and dug his heels into his gelding's flanks, whooped, and sent it charging for the shelter of the trees on the other side of the creek.

The gun roared, ripping the mountain silence apart.

Blam! Blam! Blam!

Lead hissed past Harvey. A cloud of crows whirred up out of the trees ahead, raucously cawing. They wheeled west towards the brilliant sunset.

Harvey unhooked the leather thong off the hammer of his Colt and pulled the weapon. Cocking it, he turned in the saddle and drove off two shots at where he thought the firing was coming from, hoping to make the bastard duck.

It didn't happen.

Blam! Blam!

From the corner of his eye Harvey caught the vivid orange flashes of the gun's flames as they spurted out of the greenery. More lead droned close. He hiked off two more shots – but all the time he expected to feel lead slam into him or hit, with soapy noise, the flesh of his horse. Instead, the lethal metal again snarled past to slash branches and shred leaves off the trees he was heading for.

The ambush rifle roared again. *Blam! Blam! Blam!* The vivid echoes rampaged into the mountains.

Harvey was plunging into the cover of the trees when pain seared across his upper right arm. He tried to suppress his harsh cry knowing it would send a message to that murderous bastard he was hit. As the greenery closed around him, the rifle-fire ceased abruptly and Harvey quickly came to the opinion he was up against a professional. The son of a bitch wasn't going to waste lead firing at a target he couldn't see.

But thank God for dud cartridges. He would be dead meat otherwise.

Now all he could hear was the splashing of

his burro running down the creek, the fading cries of the crows and the bickering echoes of gunfire chattering away into the snow-capped mountains. Then, silence so quiet he could hear his own ragged breathing. Gingerly, he dismounted. Thoughts of running didn't enter his thinking. He began to rearm his Colt.

Loaded, he placed the Colt in its holster and secured it with the retaining loop. Now he slid his Winchester .44 out of its saddle scabbard – always well oiled and fully loaded.

One thing was lodged in his mind. He must get that son of a bitch out into the open, cause him to make a bad move. When the idea how to do it came to him it was simple: make the bastard think he was making a run for it. He took a deep breath.

'Yeeeeehah! Hit the trail, hoss!'

He smacked the gelding twice, hard across its rump. It responded immediately, neighing its protests as it lunged into the trees and headed for the Garford Creek-Turlock trail. But he knew it wouldn't go far; it was trained. And, glory of glories, responding to his trap, the bushwhacker popped up out of the undergrowth.

His rifle was jammed into his right shoulder. Soon he was levering off, sending shots slashing through the undergrowth, chasing after the horse. But, as Harvey calculated, the lead ricocheted harmlessly off the trees, rocks and brush in its path and the horse ran on unscathed.

Burning to wreak revenge, Harvey came up out of the undergrowth. He brought up his rifle and levelled it. With deliberate intent he levered off three shots. There was a cry of pain followed by a gasp, and then the ambusher ducked low and scrambled for the cover of denser brush. Harvey followed the man's noise, scarifying the area with murderous fire. More yells of pain came before whimpering away to silence.

Harvey licked his dry lips and, with a shaking hand, dashed sweat off his forehead. He crouched and stared into the brush, blinking irritating sweat out of his eyes.

One thing was for damned sure: he wasn't going to gamble here, though he suspected the bushwhacker was badly hit. He wanted to meet this man face-to-face – to find out what was going on – but with little risk to himself. That wasn't cowardice in his book; it was commonsense.

Harvey tried to ignore his quivering limbs, the sweat running down his hard-muscled back. There was a possibility the bushwhacker was dead, but the other possibility was he was very much alive. And while that type of *hombre* was alive, he was dangerous. Most of his ilk were. Harvey knew he needed to surprise him and to do that he must come at him from a new angle.

He made an Indian-run upstream. Beyond the first bend, he crossed the brook. Without pausing, he padded back down through the aspens. A quarter of a mile on, he came up on the ambusher.

The fellow was sprawled out against a large, moss-covered boulder. He was leaking a lot of blood. His vacant black eyes were staring fixedly at a point ahead of him. His normally swarthy face was now pale yellow.

Harvey narrowed his eyelids, kept in cover. Despite the fellow's bad state he wouldn't rush into this. That kind of foolishness got a man killed. He must weigh the situation up. The fellow's left hand was pressed hard against the wound in the centre of his midriff. Blood was oozing from the injury and also from a hole in his left shoulder. Further examination revealed the man's right hand was pressed to a hole in his right thigh, which was also seeping crimson. Giving Harvey further comfort he saw the man's rifle was lying on the ground some yards from him. He seemed to have no interest in the weapon. On top of that, the ornate Mexican holster strapped to his right thigh was empty. Harvey decided it was reasonable to assume the shooter got lost in the man's mad scramble to reach safety.

Confident, he stepped out of the bushes and lined up his Winchester.

'OK, mister, you've got some talking to do.'

The fellow's reactions were rattlesnake fast. His right hand whipped down to the hidden side of his injured right leg. Almost within that same instant Harvey saw the fellow's gory paw come up filled with a Remington cap-and-ball. It boomed shockingly and Harvey felt hot lead slash across his left ear, searing him with pain as it took a piece out of the lobe. His own rifle shot, hastily made, hit the fellow's gun hand.

Sheer luck!

The fellow cried out as his six-gun went spinning. The weapon hit ground some twenty feet away. Harvey noticed his shot made bloody stumps out of the first two fingers of the fellow's right hand. He was crouching, moaning. He began rocking back and forth while holding the damaged member to his crimsoned chest. Almost cringingly he looked up, surprise in his black eyes.

41

'Why you want to kill me, gringo?' he said.

Harvey looked at him with cold eyes. 'Let's just turn that around, mister,' he said. 'Why d'you want to kill *me?*'

The 'breed – he was definitely a 'breed – shrugged. 'It is just a job, *amigo*. It is nothing personal.'

'Nothing personal, uh?'

'That is right. I do a job.'

'You don't do it very well.'

The 'breed shrugged. 'Who is to know when a cartridge is faulty?'

'Who wants me dead,' Harvey said, 'if it ain't personal?'

The 'breed looked regretful. 'Unfortunately, I cannot tell you that.'

'It's not about the money, then?' Harvey said.

The half-breed's black stare kindled with interested light and his eyelids narrowed.

'It is in the saddle-bags?' he said. 'The money?'

'You didn't know?'

The 'breed shrugged. '*Si*, but I guess. It wasn't hard.' His brown eyes now registered appeal. 'Gringo, you tell me, uh? How much? I got to know.'

Harvey offered a grim smile. It was a pleasure to inform this murderous bastard

42

what he missed out on.

'Fifty thousand dollars.'

The 'breed shook his head. *'Madre de Dios!'*

Clearly despondent he slumped back against the rock. He started breathing heavily as though the information was too hard to bear. Bubbling noises came from deep within his chest. Soon blood frothed out of the gaping wound in his midriff and dribbled from his already reddened mouth.

It was clear the man was fading fast.

'Who hired you?' Harvey said.

'Why I tell you?'

Something akin to a snarl distorted the 'breed's face and pure evil put malevolency into his eyes, new energy into his riddled body. It was with fearsome passion he screamed, *'Perdición* on your house, gringo! You ruin my dreams!'

Like a striking rattler he leaned forward. He whipped his damaged right hand behind his back. It came up holding a slim-bladed Spanish stiletto.

With a gasp Harvey threw himself sideways but despite his swift reaction the knife-edge cut a shallow gash along the right side of his neck. He felt warm blood begin to trickle.

He swung up his Winchester and fired. His bullet stamped a bloody hole into the centre of the 'breed's forehead and a mush of brains, bone and blood sprayed out of the back of the fellow's skull, splattering the mossy rock behind him. The half-breed's eyelids were now blinking rapidly as he slowly slid sideways. Harvey reckoned the man was dead before his body hit the rocky ground.

He stared down at him dispassionately.

'Just ain't been your day, *amigo*,' he said, not attempting to hide his contempt.

Slowly he lowered the smoking rifle. Curiosity demanded he allow his gaze to wander over the man's bloodstained blue silk shirt, which showed through the gap of his open, silver-studded black leather vest. Embroidered across the right breast-'pocket of the shirt were the words: *For Ramos from his darling Juanita Morales.*

'Guess you've got some mourning to do, uh, Juanita?' Harvey said.

He made the comment without emotion. It could have been him lying there and it could have been his bride-to-be, Sarah Pickett, who would have been doing the sorrowing. How could he have feelings about it?

He continued to stare at the *pistolero*. Well, one thing was for sure: he wasn't taking the 'breed back to Turlock right now. He had fifty thousand dollars to deliver.

After searching the man's pockets but finding nothing useful or incriminating, he dragged his carcase into a pile of large boulders nearby. He heaped rocks over it to keep the critters off. Then he searched for the man's horse. He found it tied up a couple of hundred yards back, up the slope amongst the aspen and pine.

He stripped it of the ornate saddle and bridle and turned it loose. But before he did, he paused a moment. Sensibly, he should follow the animal to see where it led him. But Harvey was already of the opinion its owner was an out-of-town *pistolero*, shipped in to do a job on him. Why? He had yet to find out.

He gave the animal a hard smack and sent it running into the hills. If a cougar didn't get it, it would soon find wild-horse running mates or some cowboy would pick it up. What the hell? he thought.

He turned and looked at the saddle. It was a beautiful Mexican rig, adorned with silver. The leather was intricately carved. The fellow must have spent a lot of his time in Old Mexico to own a saddle like that, as well as earned a lot of money – or thieved a lot of money. Whatever. He would take it with him when he returned to Turlock. Somebody might recognize it and give him a name.

45

But that didn't really matter either. There was a third party involved in this money deal. It could only be he who was responsible for putting the bushwhacker on to him. Why he did was for Harvey to find out. But one thing was for sure: no way could it be his pa, Sheriff Grant Watson, who loose-talked. He was as true as Toledo steel and careful to a fault.

Harvey headed for Eagle Bluff waystation, sure his friend Grover Ash would fix up his hurts. Grover was an experienced nurse-orderly who served with the Union Army during the insurgency. After the peace was signed, Grover re-enlisted, and for thirteen years he was part of the black detachment seconded to the Fifth Army in Arizona Territory, to serve under Crook. The Apache quickly christened them Buffalo Soldiers because of their kinky hair and admirable fighting qualities.

Yeah, Grover would fix him up, feed him, and certainly play some cards and find him a bunk for the night.

CHAPTER FIVE

As on the first night of his outward journey, on this return trip Harvey spent the last night in the company of Grover Ash at Eagle Bluff way station, ate venison stew for supper and played some more cards and lost some more money, but only nickels and dimes. After an early breakfast he resumed his journey. Now, at the site of the attempted ambush, he trotted the gelding to the edge of Shadow Creek and pulled rein.

His wounds were more or less healed, thanks to Grover Ash. And, better still, the rest of the ride to Garford Creek and back proved to be uneventful. Best of all, the money in the saddle-bags was now safely deposited in Garford Creek's City Bank. However, considering the circumstances, when he paid in the money, perhaps fool- ishly – he could call himself a damned fool occasionally – he passed on the envelope with the name of the depositor still sealed within it. But there was a reason for that. Part of the conditions of delivery was that the depositor's name remained secret and his strong sense of honour, instilled in him by his surrogate pa over long years, just would not allow him to take even a peek. But at the end of the day, did it matter? Grant Watson would have the name of the depositor and he was sure the sheriff would disclose that name when he heard about the attempted ambush and his surrogate son's narrow escape from death. Not only that, there was another possibility. Maybe his pa spotted the half-breed killer in town.

It would certainly account for his feeling he was being watched before he set off for Garford Creek.

He guided his steel-grey gelding into the jumble of rocks nearby, in which he buried the ambusher's body. To his complete surprise, mixed with no small anger, he found the temporary grave was empty. He dismounted stiffly and surveyed the burial place. There weren't even the remains of crushed bones to suggest coyotes, wolves, or bears got to the 'breed's carcase. He moved to where he cached the saddle. The brush he placed over the rig to hide it was thrown aside. The saddle was gone. One thing was for sure, Harvey now decided, no animal but a human would have done that. It was just one more mystery to add to the others he had encountered.

He led his horse and burro to the river's bank and allowed them to drink and then topped up his water canteens. After that he satisfied his own thirst. Remounted, he tugged the lead rope on the burro and with a click of his tongue he eased his gelding forward – down the boulder-flanked winding stage-road to the sun-baked flats below.

As before, on reaching those simmering expanses, the heat hit him with scorching intensity. Almost immediately sweat began running freely from him, but he urged himself and his animals mercilessly on.

He drank coffee at Coronado Sinks, the stage post frying halfway across the flats, topped his canteens and headed out again. More than anything he wanted the name of the third man in this deal – the man who possibly ordered his death for reasons known only to him. It was another enigma.

A slow anger was starting to burn in him. He set his jaw into a grim line and urged his gelding on.

By the time Harvey hit Turlock it was dark. He felt utterly drained. Half an hour ago, a stiff breeze sprang up. The dense clouds of sharp particles thrown up from the bed of the dry country bled his face, caused his horse and burro to lower their heads against it and snort their protests. He knew these dust storms didn't last long – that they were a local phenomenon – but while they did rage they were pure hell. He could have looked for shelter, mostly did, but this time he pulled up his bandanna and bent into it, his pure cussedness driving him on.

At the adobe sheriff's office, with its new brick-built jail house at the back, he climbed wearily down from his equally tired horse. He secured it, and the burro, to the four-horse tie-rail before the improved premises. Both animals immediately turned their rumps to the wind.

For a moment Harvey paused on the boardwalk to listen to the wind-driven grit chattering against the clapboard dwellings of old Turlock before it hissed down the rest of the rutted street into the dust-fogged darkness beyond.

The miners' part of town was half a mile up the road, beyond the old settlement. Harvey could barely see the light from the lanterns that illuminated the place, but he could hear the wind booming the canvas walls that still made up a major part of these new additions to Turlock old town. Also he could faintly hear the honky-tonk pianos jangling out their toe-tapping tunes; faintly hear the gold-loaded prospectors and the hard-rock miners in town for a good time whooping it up in the many saloons and gambling houses.

There was no doubt about it, things were going apace in this once quiet and pleasant cow-town of Turlock. There was a tremendous energy pervading the air, a confidence, a pioneering go-to-hell spirit. It was inevitable. Enterprising Eastern companies and English speculators were shipping in the hardrock men as fast as they could in order to dig and wash for gold instead of pan for it, as most of the early prospectors did and the present loners were still doing. Clearly they wanted to turn places that were pecked at up until now into profitable ventures. Indeed, there was firm opinion this was a major strike. But such things happened in the West, Harvey knew. As often as not the gold or silver so coveted by the adventurers petered out leaving only ghost towns in their wake as the Boomers and others moved on to other promising El Dorados. Not that it really concerned him. He was a cowman through and through.

Harvey stepped across the boardwalk

fronting the sheriff's office. The walkway was covered by the wooden ramada. Before the door he pulled down the bandanna he earlier placed across his mouth and nostrils to keep out the dust. But before he entered the office, he once more stared up the road as another much deeper concern built up in him. The miner's town was now the Devil's own playground and his pa was in the thick of it. Truth be known, at sixty-seven years of age and arthritic, his pa was in no shape to handle that kind of trouble any more. Harvey shook his head as the oft-of-late thought again came to him: but try telling the old cuss that.

Harvey set his jaw, more than a tad angry at the old man's continued stubbornness. He was convinced nobody would think the worst of Grant should he choose to retire. For thirty years Grant Watson had served this community well. But in the end the stubborn old mossy horn would pick his own time.

With those thoughts Harvey crossed the boardwalk and opened the office door. As he entered, dust billowed in with him and he quickly closed the door behind him. Turning, he discovered his pa wasn't at his usual place in the swivel chair behind the scarred oak desk. It was Deputy Abe Latter sitting there. He was reading the town's only newssheet, *The Turlock Echo*.

Abe rode into town four months ago. He carried impressive references as to his abilities as a lawman and, right off, Grant Watson, with the town council's blessing, swore him in. For, though gold was only discovered six months ago, in two short months lawlessness became endemic in Turlock – killings and back-alley robbery commonplace. The town council had to act.

Abe soon proved his enrolment wasn't a waste of money with shows of effective crowd handling and significant arrests. However, even with Abe's recruitment, it quickly became obvious more law was needed and three months ago Shorty Tate was enrolled on the back of Abe Latter's recommendation.

Shorty Tate was totally different. A real hard man – some said brutally ruthless – but he proved to be a very effective lawman. Harvey didn't like him. He was convinced there were the elements of a killer lurking in the man. But they hadn't manifested themselves as yet so maybe he was wrong. He was big enough to admit that, if it proved to be the case.

As Harvey turned from closing the door, Abe laid down the newspaper he was reading and gazed at him, amusement in his look.

'You look as though you've had a desert to cross,' he said.

Harvey cracked his dust-and-sweat-caked face with his own brand of smiling – he got on with Abe – and said, 'It's obvious, huh?' Then he got right down to what he was here for. 'Is Pa around, Abe?'

The deputy eased up from his lounging position. 'Haven't seen him since noon, but that don't mean much.'

He looked up at the white-faced clock with Roman numerals fastened to the far wall of the office. 'He should be at Ma Dugan's by now is my guess, being near chow time.' He grinned wryly. 'You know how Ma gives him some real earache if he don't show up on the dot.'

Harvey returned the smile and said ruefully, 'Just happy somebody can bully him.' He touched the brim of his hat. 'Well, I'll head along, Abe. It's been a long day.'

'Sure,' Latter said, and picked up the newssheet again.

On his way out Harvey paused and helped himself to a ladle of water from the bucket hanging against the street wall. As he quenched his thirst Abe said, 'If you catch up with him tell him things are fastened down tight here. No need to bother coming back.'

'If he'll listen,' said Harvey, but feeling grateful he hung the ladle on the hook provided and added, 'Thanks anyway, Abe.'

Abe waved an arm. 'Any time,' he said. 'I like the old fellow, too, you know.'

Harvey nodded. 'I have noticed.'

He stepped out of the office, once more into the darkness and swirling dust. On his way to Ma Dugan's he made a detour to leave his gelding and the burro at John 'Bone Weary' Hobson's Livery Stable, situated on the southern outskirts of the cowmen's end of the town. The burro, hired from Hobson, was paid for before he left. He now requested the gelding be groomed, bedded in a clean stall and fed good oats. After that Harvey ducked his head under Hobson's standpipe and pumped it with one hand to wash off the caked-on dust of the flats.

Bone Weary, he knew, came in with the first settlers. It was said he didn't have much of a business head and always seemed to be struggling. However, he was thorough and if he said he'd done a job, a man could take it for granted that was the solid truth. Consequently, most of the range fraternity in Sontan Basin used him for stabling needs, grain, or to just to plain pass the time with range gossip.

When Harvey was finished his ablutions Bone Weary passed him a piece of none-to-clean towelling and said, 'Hard ride, huh, Harve?'

'I've had easier.'

Harvey combed back his long black hair that curled into his neck and replaced his battered hat and put a coin in Bone Weary's hand.

'Have one on me, John.'

Bone Weary looked down at the coin, then looked up and grinned his delight.

'Man, with that kind of handout, I'll get me a bottle!'

Harvey returned the smile. 'Take it easy, huh?'

'Ain't in my nature,' said Bone Weary. 'You know that.'

Yeah, Harvey knew that. But John could handle his liquor, though his wife Rachel didn't approve very much.

He stepped out into the night. He decided, before going to Ma Dugan's, he would try Coley's Bar to see if Pa was there. It was the main meeting place for the local range men. Harvey knew the sheriff nightly made a point of stopping there on his way to his lodgings of fifteen-years' standing at Ma Dugan's popular rooming house. Pa often said Coley's Bar was a good place to pick up local information, as well as giving him an excuse to wet his whistle before supper.

Two minutes later Harvey turned into Coley's Bar. He closed the door against the dust and pulled down his bandanna.

He found the place busy and the atmosphere was thick with tobacco smoke and whiskey fumes, and there was also the constant buzz of range talk. As he booted across the rough boards several cowhands offered him a friendly 'Howdy, Harve' or a cheery wave before going back to their cards, their liquor and their chat.

There was a lack of ladies. Harvey knew most of the calico queens that once adorned Coley's establishment were now up the street and reaping the rich rewards to be earned for their favours in the miners' town. Harvey knew a lot of cowhands were bitter about the turn of events and when they came into town Saturday night there was usually a ruckus or two over whose piece of ass was whose.

Harvey sighed. Such things did not make his pa's job any easier. Only past-their-best big-bosomed Kate Nelson and Texas Lily Bowes stayed on at Coley's place. For years they'd entertained a regular clientele amongst the range boys and they considered staying on at Coley's was the only loyal and decent thing to do. But some uncharitable wits said it was because they were so ugly even the love-starved miners were reluctant to give them a second look, never mind a turn in the bed.

Harvey eased up to the bar.

'What will it be, Harve?' Frank Coley said.

'Make it the usual, Frank. Has my pa been in?'

Coley shook his head. 'Not yet.'

The saloon owner pulled a schooner of beer with a hairy, muscled arm and placed it with prideful care on the bar. Harvey nodded, paid and, with some satisfaction, took a long drink but jumped slightly as gunfire outside ripped the night apart. His gut clenched up. Was Pa still out there? he wondered.

Coley said, 'They're starting early.'

Harvey nodded, tried to relax. 'Guess they don't need a time of day.' He finished his beer and touched the brim of his sweat-greased hat. 'I'll be seeing you, Frank.'

Coley nodded, wiped the top of the bar. 'Take it easy out there, uh, Harve? It's getting to be a mighty dangerous place.'

'You don't have to tell me.'

Outside, standing on the dark boardwalk

58

again, Harvey buttoned up his denim range-coat and pulled up the deep collar against the swirling dust. Once more, fear for the old man's safety worked through him.

He needed to find his pa, have a really serious talk with him.

CHAPTER SIX

Ma Dugan's rooming house was a large white building on the quiet eastern periphery of the old town. Stepping into the limited shelter of the covered veranda that ran the length of it, Harvey beat his dusty hat against his equally dusty clothing before rapping on the outer door.

His firm knock brought Ma Dugan bustling to the fly door and main door. The doors opened to reveal a plump, motherly woman with a round, rosy face and violet blue eyes. She was well known to Harvey. In fact, she had been a mother to him until he moved out to the Crossed R at the age of twelve.

As soon as she saw him, delight filled her face.

'Harvey!' She stepped back. 'Come in,

come in!'

He moved into the long, familiar, well-lit hall. Ma Dugan busily closed the doors behind him.

'Pa about, Ma?' he said when she came to him.

The rooming-house owner shook her head firmly. 'No,' she said. Then she added, with some fierceness, 'But when he does arrive he'll be having a piece of my mind. The old fool should have retired years ago.'

'Have you tried telling him that?' Harvey said.

'I have,' Ma said, 'but does he take any notice?'

'Same for you, uh?' Harvey said with a wry grin.

Ma led him toward the kitchen, situated at the back of the big house. As they passed the comfortable lounge, Harvey could see the usual residents were relaxed in their chairs, smoking and talking, some reading books, some scanning *The Turlock Echo*. Clearly, supper was over.

As Harvey entered the kitchen the smell of apple pie baking assailed his nostrils. It was a mouth-watering aroma after days eating mostly trail-cooked fatback and beans. But the sensations of pleasant salivating didn't last long. It was the sheriff's continued absence that was now troubling him more than somewhat.

On top of being concerned for his father, he wanted the name of the third party passed on to him so he could question him – and his pa was the only one who knew it. There was also the matter of a thousand dollars in wages he was owed. He needed that in his pocket to finally get his long-held ambition underway.

Settling down in one of the kitchen chairs he said, 'I'll need a room for the night, Ma, if that's OK.'

Previously, he planned to ride back to the Crossed R as soon as he finished the delivery of the money and collected the wage due to him, but he held no doubts Slim Pickett would understand his decision to stay, considering the circumstances.

He turned to see Ma was beaming a smile. 'How about room number 7, next to your pa?'

Harvey nodded. 'That'll do fine.'

Clearly thrilled to have him stay, Ma Dugan wiped her hands on her white apron. 'So, me darling, what would you say to some apple pie while you're waiting for that old reprobate to appear?'

61

Harvey grinned. 'I was beginning to think you'd never ask.'

Ma playfully thumped his arm. 'Still the cheeky imp you are, Harvey Munson.'

'Would you have it any other way?' said Harvey.

Ma beamed her radiant smile. 'Indeed, I would not.'

She moved to select a pie. While she cut a wedge from it, Harvey found himself relaxing. There was something very solid and dependable about Ma Dugan. Why Pa didn't marry her years ago, only God knew. Perhaps, when he retired and his life wasn't on the line any more, he would.

It was a pleasant speculation.

A scratching came from the kitchen door. Frowning in Ma's direction he said, 'Have you got yourself a dog?'

Ma was placing the wedge of pie on a plate and pouring cream over it. She paused, turned and frowned. 'I have not. Why would you be asking?'

'Sounds as though something out there wants to come in,' Harvey said.

For some strange reason his body was tightening up. But even more odd, his instincts were urging him to unhook the retaining thong off the hammer of his Colt and draw it before he answered the scraping.

He crossed to the door and eased it open, careful to protect his body by using the thick doorjamb to cover him in case ... what?

He brought his gaze down expecting to see some sort of animal standing there seeking shelter from the swirling dust. But it was no creature he saw. It was his pa's bear-like, bloodied frame sprawled face down in the dust. The old man's right arm was still reaching out, the fingers scratching weakly, but at the dry ground. Incoherent gurgling noises were coming from him.

Harvey was down by his side in an instant.

'God's name, what's happened, Pa?'

It was at that moment Ma Dugan came to the door. As soon as she saw the sheriff lying there her flour-whitened hands went to her mouth and her gentle eyes rounded in horror. 'Holy Mother Mary!' She waved an urgent arm. 'Bring him in, Harvey! Bring the poor darling in! Oh, I knew it! I warned him! He wouldn't listen! Oh! Please, God, don't let the dear man die.'

Already anticipating Ma, Harvey found it took all his considerable strength to lift the big, raw-boned lawman. The necessary pressure he used to raise him caused the old man to cry out with the influx of new pain.

His yell caused anger to course through Harvey, as well as stark anguish at being the author of such agony. Meantime, Ma cleared the big kitchen table.

Harvey laid the old man as gently as he could on to it. It was then he recoiled in horror when he saw the full extent of his father's injuries. There was a severe wound in the old man's throat. There was also a big exit hole in his chest. Clearly, the bullet entered from the back. It must have been tampered with to cause such a horrendous exit hole. Bits of bone and flesh were splayed out from it in the shape of an open fan and blood was bubbling out of the gaping wound with each laboured breath. Harvey concluded it was a miracle the old man was still alive. It was an even greater marvel Grant managed to drag himself to this place. Sheer raw guts must be the only answer.

'Who did this, Pa?' he said.

A gargle came from the old man's mouth but Harvey felt his firm grasp clamp around his arm. His pa's blue stare blazed up at him in anguish. The torture in that gaze told Harvey everything about the terrible pain the old man was suffering; also told him about the frustration, the desperation the old fellow was feeling as he tried to get out a name, or tell what he knew.

Ma Dugan, who was hovering in the background, now came forward. She was wringing her hands. Then she said, as if with some amazement, 'Dear, God, what am I standing here for? It is the doctor we want.'

She began frantically peeling off her apron. A quick glance told Harvey that tears were streaming down her plump cheeks. There was also a look of tragedy in her stricken gaze. Her apron discarded, Ma went running down the hallway. Moments later Harvey heard the outer doors of the house banging to and Ma's flat-heeled shoes clumping across the veranda boards outside before fading into the dust-blown night.

Pa was tugging at his arm again. He was trying to say something, but there was just a horrible gargling noise coming out. Clearly frustrated by his inability to form words, the old lawman now began indicating he needed writing materials.

Harvey nodded his understanding and hurried into Ma Dugan's private rooms. He went straight to the bureau and pushed up the roll-top lid. Having lived here for seven years as a child, he was fully conversant with the layout of the good lady's busy establishment.

He quickly gathered a couple of sheets of notepaper and a pen. Then he lifted out the inkwell, which was countersunk into the back of the desk. He returned to the kitchen. Setting down the inkwell on the dresser he dipped the pen into it and placed it in his pa's hand before arranging the notepaper on the table surface and guiding the old man's hand over it.

'Just a name, Pa,' he said. 'Just give me a name.'

The old man's hand was shaking as he tried to summon up enough will to write all he wanted to, but despair, etched with frustration, was in every line of his face as he failed and slumped back. The pen clattered to the floor.

Harvey gazed into his pa's wide-open eyes. The vacant orbs were looking fixedly at the kitchen ceiling. The old man's mouth was trying to form words but nothing was coming out, only a trickle of blood that coursed slowly down his stubborn chin and sinewy neck. After moments he gave out a long, shuddering sigh and his dull stare anchored itself in the realm of the unseeing.

Harvey became aware that his lower lip was trembling and that a band of near unbearable heartache, like a vice of steel, was tightening across his chest. He watched the last pulses of the big vein in the old man's neck slowly cease to function. Then he swallowed hard on a throat that was now as dry as the flats he so recently crossed. And it was with some reluctance he closed down the old man's eyelids. Apart from it being the thing to do, he didn't want to watch what light remained in those once go-to-hell orbs fade and die and leave nothing but the vacuity and finality of death.

There he remained motionless, hardly comprehending what had happened, not wanting to. Then, through misted eyes, he caught the gleam of the old man's law badge. As usual, it was fastened to his leather vest, over the heart. There he was, Sheriff Grant Watson, lawman; true to all the right ideals and as good a father as any man could wish for. On an impulse Harvey unhooked the emblem of authority and slid it into his pocket.

He needed something, dammit.

CHAPTER SEVEN

How long he stood there staring down at the old man he didn't know. It was the sounds of doors opening and banging to that roused him from his deep misery. He turned. He was surprised to see solemn-faced people were gathered around the door of the kitchen. They were the guests of the rooming house. Probably made curious by the commotion, but respectfully remaining silent in deference to his grief.

Doctor John Salthouse came striding into the kitchen. His black medical bag was held in his right hand. Behind him was Ma Dugan, clearly beside herself with worry. Following her was Deputy Sheriff Abe Latter. Abe's long jawed face was etched into severe lines, obviously made so by the news of Grant's shooting.

Harvey moved aside to allow Doctor Salthouse to get near the sheriff's body. He found himself desperately nourishing the hope the sawbones would work some miracle; cause new life to enter his pa's lifeless body. He knew that was a crazy notion, but maybe a man thought such stupid things when faced with such high grief?

Doc Salthouse leaned over the still form on the table and placed a mirror over the old man's mouth and looked for signs of misting. Not finding anything he put two fingers to the big vein on the side of the lawman's bloody neck, then he placed his stethoscope to Grant's chest and listened. After moments the sawbones looked up and gravely shook his head.

'I'm afraid he's gone, Harvey,' he said.

Ma Dugan began sobbing quietly and crossed herself, but anger flared through Harvey as the doctor uttered his opinion.

'Dammit, you think I don't know that?'

'Harvey!' gasped Ma Dugan. 'The doctor is only doing his job.'

Harvey forced down his sudden burst of rage. He knew he was wrong, dead wrong, but he wasn't about to apologize.

It wasn't in him.

'That's all right, Ma,' said Doc Salthouse. 'Harvey's not himself just now.'

Deputy Abe Latter moved to the sheriff's body and stood over it. His face was grim and carved hollow in the lantern light. Harvey watched the deputy's hands slowly clench into fists until the knuckles showed white.

'No way for a man to go,' he said. His blue gaze flicked up. 'He say anything, Harve? Give a name?'

Harvey shook his head. The hot wrath that flared unreasonably through him seconds ago was now under control. As for his pa's dying: the dead were dead. Nothing and no one was going to change that. But one thing was certain. There was a killer on the loose in Turlock. He turned to Abe Latter.

'You'll be needing a deputy, Abe,' he said.

Latter's blue-grey gaze rested on him. 'You offering?'

Harvey nodded. 'I am.' He turned to Doc Salthouse. 'Will you see to Pa's needs, John – coffin and all? I'd appreciate it.'

The medic stared; there was clearly no rancour in him after Harvey's brusqueness. 'You think you need to ask, Harvey? As you well know, the sheriff was a very dear friend of mine. It will be an honour.'

Harvey nodded, thought momentarily of apologizing for his recent unwarranted outburst but didn't.

'Thank you, John,' he said.

He reached for the Colt at his right hip, replaced when he found his pa and needed to carry the old man into the kitchen.

He drew the weapon, opened the gate and spun the cylinder. He counted five bullets, one chamber left empty for the firing mechanism to rest upon to avoid accidents. He loaded the empty sixth chamber and replaced the weapon. It was well known on the range he was more than capable with Colt or rifle.

He looked at Abe Latter. 'I'm aiming to take a look out there right now, Abe. Are you agreeable?' He said it as though he was going, acceptable or not.

Latter nodded. 'The sooner the better, is my reckoning.'

Satisfaction in him, Harvey picked up one of Ma's oil lamps. He looked at the grieving rooming-house owner.

'I'll be needing this, Ma.'

The lady's tear-stained gaze came up. 'Take it,' she said. Sudden, hard flame kindled her usually kind gaze. 'Get that murdering scum, Harvey,' she said with a venom he never knew was in her. 'In the name of God, get him!'

Made sober by her fierce earnestness he said, 'If it's the last thing I do, Ma, and that's a promise.'

There was a rasping edge to his voice; a grating menace that brought narrow, searching stares from the rest of the group gathered in the doorway, even a look of wary unease from some.

He was hardly aware of them. There was a singleness of purpose in him as he walked to the back door of the rooming-house.

Abe Latter joined him and, grim-faced, they stepped out into the darkness and the dust of the back lot.

CHAPTER EIGHT

Out on Ma's back yard Harvey pulled his bandanna across his mouth and nostrils, though the wind was now abating and the dust was not so bad. Taking Ma's lamp down close to the ground he bent and observed the deep ruts left by his pa while crawling to reach Ma Dugan's back door.

The grooves ran two-inches deep through the soft dust. They were stained darkly with the old man's blood. Already the swirling dust was filling in the furrows.

Harvey spoke through his bandanna. 'Let's see where they take us, Abe.'

The deputy nodded; kept his face and his

emotions masked.

The bloody tracks led them along Turlock's twisting back alleys. Reaching the busiest livery establishment in town – Grinstead's Hay and Grain – the tracks got lost amongst a maze of hoof- and bootprints. Harvey was amazed as to how his pa found the strength of will to keep crawling while suffering such terrible wounds.

Sombre-faced he turned to Abe. 'We'd better ask at the barn,' he said. 'Maybe somebody saw what happened.'

'Don't you reckon they would have reported it by now if they had?' Latter said.

'Still figure we ought to ask,' Harvey said.

Latter shrugged. 'No harm done, I guess.'

They walked in through the narrow gap left in the big sliding doors of the stables. Inside Harvey found the hay-and-ammonia-fumed air strong. However, finding the atmosphere was reasonably free of dust he pulled down his bandanna and beat dust off his clothing. When he looked up, Harry saw the hostler Jack Smith was at the far end of the runway. He was scraping up straw and horse droppings and depositing the mixture into a high-sided wheelbarrow.

When he saw them, Smith waved a hand, apparently pleased to see them; just happy some company was arriving through the doors, thought Harvey. It was well known Jack liked to gossip.

'Well, howdy, boys,' Smith called. 'What can I do for you?' He was already walking towards them, carrying the dung fork.

'You hear shooting just now, Jack?' Harvey said when Smith arrived.

'I sure did – about half an hour ago. I was at the manure heaps out back. I finished what I was doing then came to take a look, but I didn't see a thing.'

'Nothing at all?' Abe said.

Smith nodded. 'Uh, huh. The dust was too thick, I guess, night too dark. But I didn't look too close mind – shooting going on most nights anyway.' He looked sourly at Abe.

'Just getting to be the normal thing around here, seems to me.'

Clearly stung by the suggestion that the local law was not doing its job, Latter leaned forward, his blue-grey stare mean. 'Sheriff Watson has just been murdered, Jack,' he said, 'that news change your outlook a little?'

The stableman's seamed face lost its alienation and slowly registered disbelief, then genuine regret.

'Hell, boys,' he said, 'that's a terrible thing to happen.'

74

'Yeah,' Harvey said. 'So, you still saying you saw nobody?'

The stableman assumed an injured look. 'God's truth, boys, I wish I could say otherwise, but I can't.' He added feelingly, 'Hell, I liked the sheriff– he was a real gent.'

'Think hard, Jack,' said Abe Latter. 'Try and picture what you saw when you looked out of the stable doors.'

The hostler frowned and set to scrubbing his greying beard stubble as if giving the matter heavy consideration. After moments he shook his grizzled head. 'Sorry, boys,' he said, 'all I saw was dark and dust.'

'Didn't you see the sheriff crawling away?' Harvey said.

The hostler stared his astonishment. 'Hell, Harve,' he said, 'don't you think I would have done something about it if I had?'

Harvey felt slight regret for his insensitivity and sighed. 'Yeah, I guess you would at that. Well, if you do recall anything, Jack – anything at all – let Abe, me or Deputy Tate know right away, uh?'

Smith squinted. 'You with the law now, Harve?'

'Until Pa's killer is hanging from the gallows.'

Smith shook his head. 'Goddamn it,

Harve,' he said. 'Who could have done such an awful thing?'

'That's what we aim to find out.' Harvey touched the rim of his hat. 'Well, be seeing you, Jack.'

Back in the swirling dust and darkness of the town's periphery Harvey turned to Deputy Latter.

'Look for more sign?'

Latter nodded. 'It'll be filled in if we don't.'

Harvey pulled up his bandanna and picked a spot fifty yards from Grinstead's big doors. They began rotating out, like the rings in a rock-disturbed pool. Within a minute Harvey found his pa's Star six-shooter. It was already half buried by the drifting dust. Using the light of Ma's lantern he quickly established one shot had been fired from the weapon. Calling Deputy Latter over together they made a study of the tracks his pa left, also the dark bloodstains in the immediate vicinity of the discovered Star six-shooter. Right in that spot must have been where the shooting took place, Harvey decided. The bootprints around the six-gun suggested the first shot to hit the old man – remembering the angle of the wound's entrance and exit when he examined his pa – came from behind. It looked as though the bullet entered under his left armpit, tracked across his left shoulder blade before deflecting and ripping out through his throat. Further investigation indicated his pa's other wound – when he began to turn to retaliate – entered his left side lower down, glanced off a rib, spread and exited through his sternum, missing his heart by no more than an inch. It was obvious to Harvey – judging by the horrendous wounds – that the loads that hit the sheriff were doctored to spread on impact. Further, the shock of the lead hitting his pa must have rendered him almost immobile. But the old man went down fighting, that was clear. The shot that was fired from his Star six-shooter implied nothing less.

Why his father didn't get off more shots could only be put down to the fact that his gun must have been jolted out of his hand when he fell to the ground, or shocked out by the impact of the first shot. Even so, the deep finger-scrapes Harvey could now see in the dust close by lead him to believe his pa was reaching for his six-shooter to continue to fight, savagely wounded though he was.

Deep respect in him, Harvey looked up, his face etched into severe lines. Abe Latter met his stare. It was clear the deputy also read the story in the sand. 'A real game old rooster your pa, Harve,' he said.

'They didn't come any better.'

Latter sighed. 'No.' Then he squinted. 'How do you see it now?'

'Looks to me the back-shooter was either disturbed or the old man managed to hit him with that shot he fired.'

Latter pursed his lips. 'Possible, I guess. Or the bastard figured he'd got the job done and was making himself scarce.'

'Run like a coward,' said Harvey.

'I ain't arguing,' Latter said.

They continued with the search. Some fifty yards beyond Grinstead's Hay and Grain below the down-pipe of a rundown tarpaper shack fronting a side alley, Harvey found a big water-butt. Behind it were three empty shell-cases, plus bootprints. It suggested this must have been the bushwhacker's hideout. It further indicated the killer stalked the old man before gunning him down.

Staring at the empty shell-cases Harvey said, 'Looks to me as though the bastard missed with one.'

'If you say so,' said Latter. 'I didn't get a close look at the body.'

Harvey picked up and examined the shell cases and discovered they were still slightly warm. They were standard .44s – nothing unusual in that. However, further observation revealed the boot-prints in the mud were made by flat-heeled town-wear. In addition, carved into the instep of each boot and imprinted into the sludge, was the picture of a snarling wolf.

Harvey glanced at Latter.

'Seems like we need to be looking at boots, Abe.'

Latter nodded. 'Yeah, but there's a hell of a lot of boots in Turlock right now. It'll take time.'

'Got to agree, but it don't stop us looking.'

Harvey followed the boot-tracks up the trash-filled alley. Out on to the main drag, in the miners' part of town, the tracks became lost amid the myriad of other footwear prints. Harvey stared down the street. Dust still whirled about. This part of town never slept. The oil-lamplighted main avenue was alive with horsemen. Mule-towed, fully loaded ore wagons were constantly rolling by. On top of that, reeling half-drunk hard-rock miners and grisly prospectors were moving erratically from one rip-roaring watering-hole-and-gambling-den to the next.

Harvey saw several fistfights were being fought out amid the dust and horse droppings of the main drag. And it was clear that most men participating in these inebriated brawls were so bemused by rotgut liquor that they were missing with more punches than they landed. Nevertheless, it did not stop them trying.

But tempering the raucous clamour, Harvey heard the strains of sweet music. His eyes were drawn to the spot. He observed a roughly painted board over the door of a large canvas marquee fifty yards up the street. The garish red sign above it announced it was the Grand Metropolitan Music Hall. The sounds of a woman warbling the latest soulful ballad to hit the West reached him on the dust-laden air.

Harvey pulled his gaze away from the scene. He said to Latter, 'I guess we need to pay Lucas Skinner a visit, Abe. Maybe the wolf's head motif is a trademark. Perhaps Lucas can rundown the maker and we can take it from there.'

Lucas Skinner was the town's only haberdasher and general dealer. At this moment all footwear sold in Turlock came from Lucas's rapidly expanding emporium.

'Got to be the way to go,' Latter said.

They headed into the night. But as they walked Harvey got the depressing feeling this manhunt could become a very drawn-out business, unless they hit a lucky streak, or somebody got careless, or nervy, or...

Hell, he just didn't know. And for the first time in his life he felt frustrated, inadequate and helpless – as well as grief-stricken. But then he remembered his pa's bloodied body, remembered what the man stood for, remembered what he did for this town over the years and the sacrifices he made to rear Harvey Munson and bitter determination filled him. 'Let's go see Lucas,' he said.

CHAPTER NINE

A brisk four-minute walk brought them to Lucas Skinner's two-storey dwelling. It was a large wooden building on the quiet southern edge of the old town. Like most of the old structures in the area it was painted white, with a white picket fence surrounding it. Fronting it was a house-length veranda. Hanging from hooks in the far corner was a big swing with cushions still on it. The pillows were fast gathering dust. Alice, Skinner's wife, must have forgotten to bring them in when the storm blew in.

Harvey knocked on the door and thin, hawk-faced Alice answered. She peered at them through the narrow gap she made to try and keep out the dust, which, thank God, was now abating.

'Yes?' she said.

She was clearly none too pleased to see them.

Deputy Latter took off his hat. 'We'd like to speak with Lucas, Alice, if we may. It's kind of urgent.'

Mrs Skinner's face turned waspish. 'It's late. He needs some time off. Gets none these days with that trash up there–' She waved a haughty hand towards the miners' town half a mile up the road, 'wanting this and that twenty-four hours a day.'

Harvey thought it must have escaped Alice's notice that the 'trash' were making her husband a very rich man.

'It's real important, Alice,' Latter said.

'It always is.'

Mrs Skinner sighed and appeared to relent. 'Oh, very well, you'd better come in, I suppose, if only to get the damned door shut.'

Alice Skinner led them to the small parlour, off the hallway, close by the foot of the stairs. Alice, Harvey knew, was old frontier stock. Despite her strong religious convictions and the fact she went to every Sunday meeting, the cussing came easy when she decided it was necessary.

Right now she clearly thought it was.

Alice opened the parlour door and said, 'Gents to see you,' and then went off towards the kitchen, still muttering her displeasure.

They found Lucas Skinner seated in a comfortable leather armchair. A lamp was on the small table beside him. He was reading Mark Twain's *The Adventures of Tom Sawyer*. When they entered, Lucas lowered the book and looked, with surprise, from one to the other.

'Why, Harvey,' he said, 'Deputy Latter. What can I do for you?'

Harvey didn't waste time. 'We would like you to take a look at something, Lucas, down by Grinstead's Hay and Grain.'

A frown clouded Lucas Skinner's brow. It was with apparent reluctance he put down his book on the small table near his right elbow. 'At this time of night? What could be so important, boys?'

'Sheriff Watson has been murdered, Lucas,' Abe said. 'We need your opinion on a piece of evidence.'

Lucas Skinner's lean, pale face immediately became etched with deep shock. 'Oh, my God, when? Where?'

Abe said, 'Tell you on the way, uh, Lucas?'

Skinner fumbled nervously with his jacket a moment, as if looking for something, then said, 'Well, yes, of course, boys.'

He got out of his chair. He turned and lifted a long grey duster coat off the ornate hook behind the parlour door. He drew it on over his black serge business-suit, which was shined here and there by frequent ironing. Harvey thought Lucas looked uncomfortable in the celluloid collar and black cravat he was still wearing around his scrawny neck. When he was ready he looked from one to the other and said, 'Well, let's go take a look, boys.'

Alice Skinner, Harvey found when they left the parlour, was standing in the frame of the kitchen doorway, floured arms akimbo. 'So you've dragged him out,' she said. 'Can't whatever it is wait until morning? We don't pay taxes to have our menfolk dragged out of their homes in the middle of the night.'

Lucas Skinner stared intently at his wife before he said, gently, 'Alice, Sheriff Watson has been shot dead. What these men need to know might be important in finding his killer. It's my duty to go with them and help in any way I can.'

Alice Skinner's mouth, already open and apparently making ready to volley off another scathing reply, closed quickly. Her brown eyes now expressed her horror. 'Oh, dear Lord,' she said. 'Poor Grant.'

For moments she stood staring at them in disbelief and then walked past them and opened the front door. Standing there she stared directly into her husband's smoke-grey eyes.

'Do what you have to do, Lucas,' she said, 'and don't come back until it's done, you hear me?'

Lucas smiled at Harvey then Latter. 'That's my girl,' he said proudly.

When they got outside Harvey found the air was still and everything was clear, starlit and peaceful. Five minutes later they were looking down at the boot marks around the water butt, left by ... it had to be the killer.

Harvey turned to Skinner and indicated the impressions in the mud. 'Take a look, Lucas. See what you can make of the logo.'

The general-store man bent and peered closely at the imprints. He attempted to scrape away some of the dust that had drifted into the impressions during the storm. Presently he straightened.

'Very unusual,' he said. 'Those boots certainly weren't bought at my store. Whoever is wearing them must have had them made by some specialist shoemaker, maybe Mexican. The wolf motif suggests it's some sort of personal mark.'

'Could you find out who made the boots?' said Harvey.

With some dubiousness Skinner rubbed his square chin. 'Won't be easy,' he said, 'but I have a book or two illustrating footwear trademarks and their owners. An answer could possibly lie in one of them. Failing that, there are one or two other tradesmen and boot makers I could contact over the telegraph, to get their views.'

'Will it take long?' Harvey asked.

'Two days?' Lucas said.

Harvey rubbed the stubble on his chin. 'Hmm.' It wasn't perfect, but it was better than nothing. Nevertheless he felt urged to add, 'It would help if you could hurry it up a little, Lucas.'

Skinner hunched his shoulders. 'I'll do my best, of course, but these things do take time. They can't be rush–'

A gun roared twice – harsh twin echoes that ripped the dark night apart. Lead hissed by with spiteful noise. Skinner yelped and Harvey blew out Ma's oil lamp and dropped into the mud around the water butt, dragging Lucas down with him. Abe Latter was already crouched against the water butt peering into the night, his Colt Peacemaker out of its holster and cocked for instant action. A deathly silence now clamped down around them.

Presently, when no more lead was forthcoming, Harvey said, 'What do you think, Abe?'

Latter shook his head. 'Beats the hell out of me,' he said. Then he added, as if it was a concerned afterthought, 'Shorty Tate's patrolling up there. It could be he's in trouble. Maybe I should take a look.'

Again Harvey thought about Shorty Tate, the other deputy on Turlock's law enforcement payroll, the one he didn't like. But he did concede Tate was a capable operator in a tight corner. However, Harvey also recalled, his pa had said Tate could be overzealous in his use of the big Colt Dragoon he carried in his belt. It was said it seemed to give Tate real pleasure to beat a man over the head with it, thus rendering him senseless. Tate's reply as to why he did this was simple: it made his prisoners much easier to handle.

Harvey narrowed his eyelids. When he first met Tate he found the man's nickname was a gross contradiction. Shorty stood at least six feet three inches tall and was built like a Brahma bull. Another striking thing about the deputy was the colour of his eyes. They were sapphire blue – cold as ice.

He said to Latter, 'Don't want to contradict you, Abe, but I reckon that shot was meant for us.'

Latter stared at him. 'But, that makes no sense at all, Harve.'

'Pa's killing didn't either.'

Latter pursed his lips. 'True enough, but it's my gut feeling Shorty's in trouble. I reckon I should take a look. In fact, it's my duty to.' The deputy's stare lingered. 'Could I leave you to get Lucas home safe?'

'You figure I can't?'

'No, but it'll take the weight off me.'

'Consider it done.'

Latter nodded then glanced from one to the other before hunching down and jogging off into the night. As the deputy faded into the darkness more shots rang out. However, this time no lead came their way.

Harvey relaxed a little. Maybe Latter was right. Maybe it was just some drunken miner letting off steam, or causing trouble. He looked about him. Now the dust storm was over the air was still and the stars were bright in the night sky above the canvas and tar-paper roofing of this now sprawling town of Turlock.

Lucas Skinner said tentatively, 'I'd like to get home, Harvey. Got a long day tomorrow.' He added, 'Of course, if I were armed, I'd do it myself, you understand. But seeing as I'm not...'

Harvey drew his long-barrelled Colt.

'No need for explanation, Lucas, just stay close.'

But cutting into his words again gunfire ripped the night. Skinner gave out a harsh cry and crumpled into the mud around the barrel. He gasped, 'I'm hit, Harve.'

Astonishment rendered Harvey immobile for a couple of seconds. Then he crouched down beside Lucas and attempted to cover him with his own body. Guilt was already thick within him. Dammit, only moments ago he was asked to protect the haberdasher. His failure to do so now hit hard.

'Where?' he said.

'Chest. High up.'

'Can you hang on?'

'I'll try.'

The sounds of more gunfire slammed into the air, more lead hissed close. It was coming from the dark maw of an alley fifty yards away. Harvey lined up the Colt and fired three shots into it. His answer came swiftly. Two shots; then – surprisingly – the sounds of a man's retreating footfalls clattering through empty food cans and other clutter as he moved up the alley.

Frustration surged through Harvey because he couldn't do a damn thing about it. He needed to stay with Skinner. But he unleashed his last two shots after the retreating ambusher. His lead clattered across the faces of clapboard buildings lining the alley then whined eerily into the night. Now silence, except for the distant hubbub of seething humanity enjoying itself coming from the miners' town.

Harvey wiped sweat off his chin with a shaky hand and then punched empty shell-cases out of his six-shooter and reloaded.

He wanted like hell to give chase, but Lucas Skinner's welfare must be his first priority. He looked down anxiously at the haberdasher. The man was clearly in pain. 'Can you walk, Lucas?'

'I'll try.' Skinner gamely attempted to get to his feet, but slumped to the ground again, sighing in his defeat.

'It don't look like it,' he said.

Skinner then seemed to faint, go limp.

Harvey reached out and opened his coat to try and ascertain the severity of his wound. But it was the harsh demand from behind that startled as well as bemused him.

'Stay real still, Harve. Throw your Colt.'

The click of a gun hammer being fully cocked came.

Harvey froze. He immediately recognized Deputy Shorty Tate's gravely voice and he quickly came to appreciate his compromising position – crouching over Lucas Skinner, smoking Colt in hand, looking as if he was searching Skinner's vest pockets.

He said, 'It isn't what it seems, Shorty.'

Tate sniggered. It sounded like a donkey braying. 'Sure it ain't, Harve,' he said. 'You're just an angel of mercy. That right?'

Harvey attempted to turn. 'Damn you, Shorty,' he began, but Tate's snarled order stopped him.

'Stay as you are, Harve.'

The Crossed R foreman froze.

Tate said, 'Better. Now, I'll ask you again – throw your Colt.'

Hot anger rose in Harvey. 'Hell's fire!' He pointed frantically at the dark maw of the alley the ambusher was making his escape up. 'There's a God-damned bushwhacker getting away from here right now – get after him for God's sake!'

'You telling me what to do?' Tate said.

'I'm telling you what's happened. Do it.'

Harvey flinched as lead kicked up sludge, close to his right boot. Again Tate's snigger came. 'Guess you didn't hear me right the first time, uh, Harve?' he said. 'I said drop your weapon. Now you do it!'

Frustration surged through Harvey.

'You've got this all wrong, dammit.'

'The weapon!' Tate said.

Once more lead splattered mud near Harvey's right boot, close enough for him to feel the vibrations of the impact through the wet soil. With some reluctance and a great deal of anger he tossed the gun.

'Man, this is crazy,' he said.

'Sure it is. Now turn ... easy.'

Harvey rose from beside Skinner and swivelled on his left boot-heel and met Tate's blue stare level on. 'If you ain't noticed,' he said, 'Lucas needs medical attention, urgently.'

'He'll get it,' said Tate. 'But, I got to say, you sure are some humdinger – ordering the law about like you done, pretending you is the injured party. Why, it looks to me you're just a God-damned back-shooting son of a bitch. By God, who'da thought it? Almighty ramrod of the Crossed R!'

Then Tate's gun arm lifted high. Harvey knew he should have anticipated the move but the deputy moved fast for a big man. He tried to avoid what was coming, but was way too late. The heavy Colt Dragoon crashed down across the side of his head. A deep black pit opened up and he tumbled head first into its Stygian depths.

CHAPTER TEN

Harvey came back to consciousness to find himself on a cell bed. Even though this was the new jail-house, the old drop-down bunks were transferred here and were still familiar to him. He spent quite a piece of his young life in his pa's old calaboose, sleeping on one or other of the cell beds when, after schooling, he grew tired of waiting for his pa to finish up and take him home to Ma Dugan's.

He lifted his head. Pain thundered like a herd of stampeding buffalo across his skull. He groaned. He gingerly felt at the crusts of blood congealed on the side of his head before glancing through the cell window bars above his head. He was surprised to see it was daylight.

He must have been out for hours.

With some effort he eased himself up off the bunk and sat on its edge and tried to ignore the pain still throbbing in his head. What was he doing in here? Then it all came back, starting with the High Tips ambush, then the events upon hitting town: his pa's brutal death; the snarling wolf imprint in the mud by the barrel outside Grinstead's Hay and Grain; the inexplicable attempt on Lucas Skinner's life – maybe *his* life, rationally thinking – then Shorty Tate whacking him over the head, clearly suspecting he was the man who shot Lucas Skinner.

He rose from the bunk and shuffled to the cell bars but regretted it immediately as more agony drummed across his skull. He did his best to ignore the pain and think straight. For sure he needed to do that.

First priority must be to get out of here. He must get after his pa's killer and the man who shot up Lucas Skinner. Maybe it was the same man? He now harboured more than a sneaking suspicion it was. And perhaps he was also Lucas Skinner's murderer now? Lucas was certainly in a bad way the last time he saw him and could be dead. But there was an even bigger mystery: why was he still in jail? Abe Latter should have dealt with Shorty Tate's stupidity soon as he knew about it and got him out of here.

'Abe!' he yelled.

The effort he put into the shout caused new pain to jar through him. A minute passed before Shorty Tate opened the substantial door leading to these new brick-built cells and leaned on the threshold, grinning at him. His bald head was mottled with sweat, his round red face even more richly hued with blotches of purple, which suggested a debauched life. 'He ain't around,' Tate said, still grinning. 'He's gone to tell Mrs Skinner you shot her husband.' Then he tittered like a schoolboy. 'Jesus, how about that?'

Harvey stared. 'He's *what?*'

'He figured it was his duty,' Tate said, his smile leaving him to be replaced with mock gravity. 'It's one of the bad sides of keeping the law – telling folk. Didn't your late pa tell you about that, Harve?'

The Crossed R foreman made an effort to calm himself. This addition to Turlock's police force was one hard-ass son of a bitch.

'Is Skinner still alive?' he said.

'He's in a coma,' Tate said, 'though Doc Salthouse doesn't expect him to come out of it.' The deputy shook his head, even sighed,

95

as if in sympathy. 'Goddamn it, Harve, you could be facing a murder charge here. Now, ain't that a turn up for the book, you being Grant Watson's son and foreman of the Crossed R and a big ass son of a bitch to boot?'

Harvey gripped the bars, warm anger slowly rising in him. 'Have a care how you use my father's name, mister.'

'Oh, I will,' said Tate. 'Truth be known, I'm real shook up about your pa's shooting – me being a lawman too. Just don't know when it's going to happen to you, uh?'

'You still trying to make this charge stick?' Harvey said.

'No choice, Harve,' Tate said amiably. 'Caught you red-handed.'

'I was protecting Skinner, not killing him.'

A sneer spread across Tate's face. 'Sure you were,' he said. 'But the way I saw it you were crouching over Skinner, smoking gun in hand, your other hand searching through his pockets.'

'I was checking on his wound, dammit!'

'My ass,' said Tate. 'You were getting ready to rob him.' The deputy paused, put a thoughtful finger to his lips. 'Or maybe you were about to shoot him dead before you robbed him? Kind of finish the job first, uh,

seeing as you didn't do it right first time?'
Tate gave out with a heavy sigh. 'Why dammit, Harve, it's beginning to look real bad for you, I got to say.'

Harvey gripped the bars, his anger flaring again. 'I told you I was—'

'Yeah, checking his pulse.' Tate folded his arms. 'I guess you'll have to tell the judge that, uh, Harve? But I figure he won't be taking a deal of notice when we give him all the facts.'

'Damn you, Tate, for a thick-headed son of a bitch! There's a killer out there! Get after him!'

Tate raised his thick black brows. 'Why? I reckon we got him right here.'

He turned and went out of the cellblock guffawing, slamming the door loudly behind him. Harvey sat down on the bunk and leaned his back against the hard brick of the cell wall. He forced himself to calm down and think. Abe Latter. Abe was a reasonable man. All he needed to do was wait until Abe came back from Alice Skinner's. Abe would soon get this whole matter cleared up.

But why didn't the deputy take issue with Tate as soon as he got to know he was in jail? Harvey shook his head in puzzled disbelief but regretted the move as more pain bounced across his skull and waves of nausea made the opposite wall go in and out of focus and the cell swim before his eyes.

He groaned. Dammit, it must have been one hell of a belt Tate gave him. But then, that Colt Dragoon Tate carried was a heavy weapon – you could say built for the job. Not only that, if you could hold the six-shooter firm and shoot it straight it could do a hell of a lot of damage to a man, outdated though the cap-and-ball pistol might be in this modern age of cartridges.

But Tate didn't use the Dragoon for killing a man. The Smith & Wesson double-action Russian he carried, set in the cross-draw position on his left hip, was there to do that job. And it was said Tate could turn into a killer at the drop of a hat. Only last week a drink-crazed miner set to shooting up the Daisy May Saloon – bullets flying every-where. The incident was reported in *The Turlock Echo*. Tate apparently warned him to stop. When he didn't, the deputy shot him dead. Didn't attempt to maim. Just shot him: *dead*.

Fresh waves of nausea undulated across Harvey's vision. Tired, he lay back on the bunk and closed his eyes and waited for the fuzziness to clear. It didn't and he drifted into restless sleep.

'Harve?'

The voice was faint, in the distance, and slow to penetrate his muss-filled consciousness. When he did open his eyes to gaze through the cell bars he saw Abe Latter was standing the other side of them.

'Shorty said you wanted to talk,' Abe went on.

'He said right.'

Harvey fought his way back to full cognizance. When he felt able to he got up off the cell bed, crossed to the bars and gripped them to stop himself falling over. He said, 'Get me out of here, Abe, dammit.'

What appeared to be genuine regret filled Latter's long face. 'Wish I could, Harve.' He sighed heavily. 'I know this'll not make a lot of sense to you but Shorty reckons he saw you shoot Lucas.'

Harvey glared. 'You know he's a damned liar.'

'Well, I do find it hard to believe,' said Latter. 'But Shorty is a fellow peace officer. I have to go along with his assessment of the situation as he saw it at the time. However, don't worry about it. I doubt the allegation will stand up in open court and I will certainly testify on your behalf.'

Harvey stared, hardly believing what he was hearing. 'Abe,' he said, 'this is crap and you know it. Goddamn, are you siding with Tate?'

Latter shook his head. 'I'm not siding with anybody.'

'Abe,' Harvey said, 'all you got to do is open the door! Be reasonable.'

'It's not as easy as that.'

'It is to me!' Harvey paused and sighed. Pain was still beating with sledgehammer force inside his head. He calmed himself. 'Abe, ask yourself this question. Why would I want to kill Lucas? Up to now he's the only man that can point us in the right direction to find Pa's killer.'

Latter's stare was level and equable. 'You think I haven't figured that out for myself?' He made a conciliatory gesture. 'Look, Harve, I'll have a talk with the town council. Maybe I can get you out on bail.'

'Bail?' Harvey said. 'Dammit, Abe, I'm innocent!'

Latter said, a little impatiently, 'Do you want me to try, or don't you?'

At that moment the deputy looked prepared to walk out of the cellblock and to hell with it. Not wanting that, Harvey composed himself. 'Abe.' He waved an arm towards the cell window, 'The killer of my father is out there. I got to get out of here. I got to go after him.'

Latter's blue-grey stare was hard-edged. 'You figure you got a monopoly on that requirement, Harve?'

Harvey sighed. 'Dammit, you know what I mean.'

The deputy studied him. After what appeared to be considerable mental deliberation he said, 'I'll send word to the Crossed R. Slim Pickett has weight in this town. Maybe he will be able to do something.'

Harvey shook his head. He didn't want Slim involved; the Crossed R owner had enough problems of his own.

'Out of the question,' he said.

Latter looked puzzled. 'Surely Slim will want to be in on this? You're going to be his son-in-law pretty soon, aren't you? And how about Sarah, your bride-to-be? She'll want to know. Hell, man, it's only right.'

Harvey said, 'I want them left out of it.'

Latter sighed and shook his head. 'You're not making a lot of sense, Harve. Slim is the one man that can maybe swing this for you. He still carries a lot of weight in this town.'

Harvey hit the bars with a hard fist. 'Abe, I shouldn't be in here, dammit. That's the

101

bottom line for me. Now, have a serious talk with Shorty and try and get him to see some sense.'

Latter pursed his lips, shook his head. 'That won't be easy. I've known Shorty a long time. For him, the law will have to run its course. That's how he is and he won't stray from that. I'm sorry, Harve.'

There was one other possibility and Harvey wondered why he didn't think of it at the start of this conversation.

'Is Lucas Skinner talking yet?'

Latter shook his head. 'No. I wish I could say he was. It'd solve a lot of problems. But he's still unconscious. He's lost a lot of blood and has a bad fever, due to the shock of the wounding. Doc Salthouse said it could be a couple of days before he comes out of it and maybe another day before he'll be able to say anything rational. And that, of course, will depend on whether he survives.'

For the first time in his life Harvey felt helpless, out of control. He stared through the bars, his desperation bright and alive. 'Look, Abe, somebody killed my pa and shot up Lucas. I think it's the same man. Don't ask me how I come to that opinion, I can't give you a rational answer. It's just a hunch. But I figure when Lucas Skinner got shot the bastard was really after me.' He tightened his grip on the bars. 'Abe, for God's sake, let me out of here.'

Latter looked regretful. 'I can't do that, Harve, wish I could. Look, I've spelled out your options. I can get you bail or I could send word to the Crossed R to come in and put on some pressure. Which one will it be?'

Maybe he was being dogmatic about bail? Harvey thought. He could be bull-headed, that was well known. He racked his brains. It wasn't long before he came up with one more possibility.

'Abe, with Pa dead, don't that make you acting sheriff – you being the longest serving? Can't you override Tate and get me out of here that way?'

Latter shook his head, even offered a wry grin. 'Man, you never give up. But the fact is any appointment has to be ratified by the council and I'm powerless to do anything until that is done. And there is always the possibility Shorty will get the job. You thought of that?'

'In a coon's age,' said Harvey. 'Unless those sons of bitches on the council have gone plumb *loco*.'

The deputy's gaze appraised him. 'Believe me, Harve,' he said, 'I want you out of here just as much as you want it for yourself A man with your incentive and intelligence has got to be a big player in catching the man that's done this.' Latter paused, rubbed his chin. 'Look, leave it with me. I'll do the best I can.'

Latter left the cellblock, closing the door quietly behind him. Harvey stared after him. It wasn't what he wanted but there was little he could do about it. But he was surprised by Latter's correctness regarding the letter of the law. He had him down as being more adventurous than that.

Again wooziness overtook him. He lay down. Damn Tate and his damned head-busting techniques.

But there would be a reckoning.

CHAPTER ELEVEN

'Chow.'

The gravel-voiced word roused Harvey from deep sleep. He felt better for his slumbers. It was nature's way of healing, his surrogate father always suggested. But raising his head sent more pain jarring through him, although it wasn't so intense this time. He stared through the cell window. It was dark outside. He swivelled his gaze now and stared through the cell bars at Shorty Tate.

'Abe Latter back?' he said.

Tate gave him a fat-faced grin.

'Impatient, uh?' Tate said. 'He told me about you wanting out. A snowball's chance in hell I'd say.'

The beefy deputy slid a wooden tray under the cell bars. On it, Harvey observed, was a chipped enamel plate filled with steak, onions and potato fries – all swimming in thick gravy. A scarred enamel mug filled with treacly-looking coffee was standing next to the plate.

The sight of the food made Harvey realize how hungry he was. He recalled his last meal was yesterday morning in the company of Grover Ash at Eagle Bluff waystation back in the High Tip foothills. Flapjacks and wild honey, beans, bacon and coffee you could stand a spoon up in. He picked up the tray.

Tate tittered and said, 'Don't go choking on it now. We want to keep you alive and well for the hanging.'

He left the cellblock guffawing.

Harvey stared at Tate's back – bull-broad at the neck and shoulders, fat about the hips: one mean son of a bitch.

Harvey gingerly fingered the scalp wound and the lump on his temple and continued his last thoughts before sleep. Yeah, he owed Tate, *big time*. He placed the coffee on the floor to drink later and began to eat the meal. The steak, he found, was as tough as buffalo hide but he chewed on it patiently. The fries and onions looked appetizing but were made to taste of axle-grease by the thick brown gravy that was slopped over them.

He was bringing the sixth forkful of food to his mouth when the Colt dropped in through the window bars behind him and clattered on to the concrete floor. Following it came a hoarse, obviously disguised, whisper: 'When you get out, a horse will be saddled and waiting for you down in the cottonwoods by Marsh Creek.' The stream, Harvey knew, came out of the Bad Back Hills and flowed across the long basin before making a big loop around Turlock prior to getting soaked up ten miles into the thirsty flats beyond.

Curious and made wary by the abrupt arrival of the weapon, Harvey put his meal aside and got up. He paced across to the cell window and used the bars to pull himself up. He peered over the window's horizon and stared out. The dark alley, he saw, was deserted but he could hear the sound of footfalls receding into the night.

He dropped back to the floor again and picked up the six-gun. He inspected it carefully. It was a long barrelled cap-and-ball Colt Army in good condition. It was fully loaded. A suggestion of excitement tingled through him, but his natural suspicion of all things odd tempered his elation. This invitation to escape could well be a trap. But then, it could be a friend who wanted to remain anonymous. He did have friends in Sontan Basin. A lot. At least he thought he did.

He settled down on the bunk again, careful to place the weapon where it could not be seen from the cell door should somebody came in unexpectedly. He completed eating his meal. By the time he finished and returned the cup and plate to the tray, a plan was formed in his mind.

He waited for the deputy to return.

Five minutes later, Tate came in, a big grin on his face. When he saw the empty plate and cup on the tray he said, 'Good to see you haven't choked on it. Pass the tray under the bars.'

Harvey lined the Colt Army up on Tate's belly button. 'Right, you son of a bitch, hoist your hands.'

If Tate was scared, he didn't show it. Slowly he elevated his arms and grinned, as if in some quirky way he was perversely delighted by what he saw.

'Well now, what have we here?'

Harvey got up and moved forward and reached through the bars and relieved the deputy of the big Dragoon cap-and-ball six-shot he carried. Using his left hand he pushed the heavy gun into his belt, keeping the Colt Army in his right hand and trained on the deputy's midriff.

He saw that Tate wasn't wearing his Smith and Wesson double-action. Harvey thought that a pity. Matched against the cumbersome Dragoon the Russian was a much more effective weapon to have – deadly in a gunfight where a quick draw was required. 'Where are the keys?' he said.

'In the office,' said Tate. He tittered. 'You figure for one moment you're going to get away with this, Harve?'

The Crossed R foreman waved the Colt towards the office.

'Anybody in there?'

'George Foley,' said Tate. 'He came in to jaw for a spell.'

Foley was the scrawny bartender at the Painted Lady, the rival saloon to Coley's Bar in the old part of town. George, as every-body knew, was the town's gossip. Harvey extended his thoughts into speech.

'Come to see if it's right the sheriffs son is in the calaboose, right?'

Tate winked. 'You've hit it, Harve,' he said. 'George brought a bottle along, too, of course.'

Harvey nodded. 'Of course,' he said, 'and thanks for telling me. It could have been real tricky, getting the keys in here from the office with nobody in there to ask, wouldn't you say?'

Tate immediately recognized his mistake.

'Goddamn!'

'Not so bright now, uh, numb head?' Harvey said. He waved the Colt. 'Right, call him. Tell him to fetch the keys.'

Tate leered. 'Suppose I don't?'

Harvey cocked the Colt Army menacingly. 'Then I'll break both your legs and take my chances.'

Tate's lids narrowed over his sapphire-blue eyes. His face went serious. He hesitated, as if he was weighing up the possibility of get-ting away with it if he challenged Harvey's threat by doing nothing, or tried to make his escape. After moments the deputy offered Harvey a sickly grin and said, 'Yeah, reckon you would at that.'

Harvey said, 'You'd better believe it.'

Tate turned his head slightly, but kept his eyes on Harvey. 'George, come on in here if you want to see Munson first-hand – and fetch the cell keys.'

'The cell keys?' George called, as if uncertain.

'You deaf or something?'

'Jesus, no, just surprised, Shorty. You letting him out?'

'No.'

'So, where are they?'

'Desk drawer, top left.'

Seconds later George Foley came into the cell extension. As soon as he saw the situation his face dropped.

'Oh, Jesus,' he said.

Harvey smiled. 'Step right in, George, and raise your hands.'

The barkeep elevated his arms with alacrity. The cell keys jangled in his right hand as his hands went toward the flyspecked ceiling.

'Don't do nothing crazy, Harve,' he said. 'You know I don't carry a gun.'

Harvey waved the Colt.

'Bring the keys over here, George.'

Foley licked his lips, flicked an anxious glance at Tate. 'What shall I do, Shorty?

Goddamn, I didn't bargain for this.'

'Just do as he says, George,' said Tate. 'Our friend is holding all the aces, wouldn't you say?'

'Yeah, yeah,' said Foley. 'I guess he is.'

The barkeep paced forward nervously and handed over the keys. As he took them, Harvey turned to Tate.

'OK, which one is the cell key?'

'The largest one,' Tate said. His round red face crinkled up, expressing mock curiosity. 'Hell, Harve, d'you really expect to get away with this?'

Harvey ignored him. He waved the Colt. 'Step back against the wall, both of you.' Foley obliged with alacrity but Tate eased back, a sneer adorning his full lips, and leaned casually against the brick wall. Harvey selected the key for the cell door, opened it and stepped out and moved to one side and waved the Colt.

'OK, get in. Both of you.'

Foley scuttled past him, hands still held high, his face pale. But Tate hesitated and for the first time looked uneasy. He eyed the weapon in Harvey's hand. 'What are you fixing to do with the Colt, Harve?' he said.

'You're wondering about that, huh, Shorty?'

Tate licked his fat lips. Sweat began to stipple his brow and bald pate and a twitch started in the corner of his right eye. He edged cautiously sideways, to go through the door.

'You try anything crazy, mister,' he said, 'and, by God–'

At that moment Harvey struck. A blur of movement and Tate let out a harsh cry as the Colt Army's barrel hammered down against his left temple. The beefy deputy went down like a sack of potatoes. Without mercy Harvey bent and hit him once more as he tried to get up.

Harvey stared down at the unconscious figure, sprawled out on the floor, blood running from his temple, and then he leaned over and wiped the gore off the barrel of the Colt, using Tate's shirt as a towel.

'Touché, Shorty, wouldn't you say?' he said.

He turned to see Foley cowering against the far cell wall, under the barred window. 'Jesus, Harve, you ain't going to do that to me, are you?'

Harvey smiled reassuringly. 'Hell no, George, but with Shorty here...? Well now, that's a different matter entirely, wouldn't you say?'

'Sure, sure,' Foley said. 'He's always too handy with that Dragoon of his.' The barkeep gestured with a thin arm. 'I tried to tell him but you know how he is.'

'Guess I do,' Harvey said. He grinned. 'Right, George, I want you to take off your belt.' Foley frowned.

'Huh?'

'The trouser belt,' Harvey said. 'Take it off.'

'Christ, what for, Harve?'

Harvey swivelled his Colt Army, cocked it, and levelled it on the thin-faced barkeep's belly button. 'George, I haven't the time for debate. Get the damned belt off. OK?'

Foley stared with ever more frightened eyes at the menacing Colt and then unbuckled his belt and allowed his trousers to drop around his ankles. His dirty red long johns were exposed to the world.

'Step out of the trousers, George.'

Foley complied.

Harvey de-cocked the Colt Army and tucked it into his waistband. He stepped forward and took the belt off the barkeep. Then he kicked George's scrawny legs from under him and the barman hit the concrete floor with a bony rattle.

Harvey then bent quickly and placed the

113

belt around the 'keeper's ankles and drew the leather through the buckle. The big anklebones crashed together and George yelped his pain.

'Jesus, Harve, take it easy!'

Ignoring him Harvey forced a new hole through the leather and secured the belt and said, 'You got a handkerchief, George?'

'Top vest pocket.' Foley squinted quizzically. 'What for?'

'A gag, George.'

Harvey reached for and got Foley's handkerchief. It was once white but was now a dirty grey. Foley was protesting, 'Jesus, Harve, there ain't no need for this. I won't call out, I'll give you my word on that. Why, dammit, every right-thinking man in this town knows you had nothing to do with Lucas Skinner's shooting. It just doesn't make a mite of sense. Everybody's saying it.'

'So, why am I in jail, George?'

Foley looked sick. 'Shorty said procedure. Said you've got to have procedure.'

'Procedure, huh?' Harvey said. 'How about my pa? Was his shooting just procedure?'

'A God-awful thing, Harve, so help me,' said Foley. 'Why, the whole town's grieving over that. Got to be some dirty yellow back-shooting coward that done it. Only way they

114

could have got your pa, I do declare.'

'And that's the reason why I got to get out of here, George,' Harvey said. 'Can't get the son of a bitch that done it sitting in here.'

'I appreciate that, Harve,' said Foley. 'I surely do, but gagging me?'

Harvey stuffed the grubby handkerchief into Foley's mouth, cutting off any more pleas. Then he tightened his own sweat-stained bandanna across the rag, effectively quietening the barkeep.

Harvey now unbuttoned the canvas suspenders supporting the unconscious Shorty Tate's trousers. Using them he secured Foley's arms behind his back and then stepped back to admire his handiwork before he turned to Tate.

He strongly suspected the deputy sheriff would be out of it for some time, the beating he gave him. Nevertheless, he looked around. He saw wrist-irons hanging from a hook cemented into the outside cell wall; manna from heaven. He took the cuffs and secured Tate to the cell bars and then fumbled through the deputy's pockets. He came up with a filthy red polka-dot hand-kerchief. He stuffed the rag into Tate's mouth and then used his own handkerchief to prevent the deputy spitting it out. Harvey now dug the Colt Army out of his waistband and crossed to the open door leading into the law office. Though it was cumbersome, the weight of the Colt Dragoon parked in his belt felt even more reassuring.

At the office door's threshold he paused, every nerve in him alive and primed for what danger, if any, lay ahead. He used the thick angle of the doorjamb for protection as he held the Colt by his right ear, ready to level up and fire if needs be. He peered into the office. A careful survey of the place, lit by the pale yellow glow of the oil lamp sitting on the desk, told him the room was empty.

He stepped across the uneven board floor and quickly doused the lamp. Then he stared anxiously through the dusty windows at the dark street beyond.

Now came the dilemma. What to do? Stay in town and try and find his pa's killer? He was convinced the perpetrator was still in the settlement. On the other hand he could wait for Abe Latter to return from Doc Salthouse's place and find out if Lucas Skinner had returned to consciousness and cleared his name. Or, better still, he could go to Doc Salthouse himself and find out that way.

Harvey crossed the dark office. He eased the door open a fraction and peered out:

116

still as a tomb – the sheriff's office, being located in the old part of town, made it so at this late hour. All the noise of mayhem was coming from the miners' sprawl a quarter of a mile up the road.

Harvey licked his lips. Sweat was trickling down his forehead and back. Making matters worse he was getting these uncomfortable perceptions again. This whole thing didn't sit right; didn't feel right. It was too easy, too convenient – the gun through the window, the horse waiting down by Marsh Creek, Shorty Tate capitulating so easily. Damn, it held all the hallmarks of a setup.

He set his jaw into a hard line and swallowed on his dry throat and stepped out into the night – into the deep shadow made by the wooden ramada above the boardwalk.

The crack of a discharged rifle came from the alley across the wide main street. In the same instant lead ripped shards of wood out of the jamb near his head. He damn well knew it! He went into a crouch, popped off two shots before running for the side street that went down past the sheriff's office and cellblock. As he turned into the alley, lead screeched across the brickwork above his head before ricocheting into the night. But, oddly, he felt elation. Once again his hunch proved right.

Harvey turned, fired again hoping it would hold the son of a bitch and give him precious seconds. But where was he to go? He now possessed few doubts that if he headed for Marsh Creek he would run into another ambush. More annoying tin cans and other trash rattled under his boots as he blundered down the alley.

The racket brought more gun reports, the buzz of lead ripping the night around him apart. One piece of shot plucked at his denim jacket, another his trouser leg. His anger hit the back of his throat. He turned and emptied the rest of the bullets in the chambers of his Colt Army into the alley across the street.

He needed to get out of town. He needed to get to his horse. As far as he could assess, it was his only chance.

He headed across the back lots. John Hobson's Livery Stable, he found, was still open. He was out of breath. He tried to control his breathing. As he eased through the big doors Bone Weary came out of the small side office and peered at him through the yellow gloom. Only three lanterns lit the premises – one at the top end of the runway, one at the bottom end, and one in the office.

Hobson smiled. 'Hey, Harve! They let you out, uh? Damn right, too. Never heard such a thing. That Shorty Tate, he must be crazy.'

'Where's my gelding, John?' Harvey said.

Bone Weary waved an arm. 'Why, right-hand bottom stall, groomed, oat-fed like you asked. You leaving?'

Harvey moved quickly down the runway. He hauled his blanket and saddle off the side of the stall. The steel-grey nickered as soon as he recognized him. He dropped blanket and rig over its broad back and cinched up.

'That shooting back there,' Bone Weary was saying, baggy eyelids screwed up, 'you involved in that?'

'Miners' shindig is my guess,' Harvey lied. He didn't like fibbing to Bone Weary but figured, the way things were, the less the hostler knew the better.

'Crazy sons of bitches,' Hobson said. 'You be heading for the Crossed R, Harve?'

'What d'you think?'

Bone Weary grinned sheepishly. 'Yeah, I guess so. Want to get out of this crazy town, uh?'

The boom of a Colt set all the horses in Hobson's place rearing and kicking and neighing. Dust sprinkled down from the haylofts above. An inch above Harvey's head lead whined off the upright, ripping out bright splinters.

Bone Weary yelped and hit the straw and horseshit belly down and flattened against it. 'Jesus, Harvey, what in tarnation is going on?'

'Keep your head down, John.'

Harvey upped the Colt Dragoon and boomed off two shots. Then he swung up on to his steel-grey's back, kicked flanks and headed for the open rear doors of the stables.

More crashes from a Colt flatted into the night and more lead blasted dust and slivers of wood from the livery barn's rear doors as Harvey high-tailed through them, the hoofs of his horse kicking up dung and dust.

Out on the starlit flats he swung the beast northwest.

He possessed no plan. He would have to play it by ear. He was a fugitive now. But two things were for sure – he didn't like running and he didn't like having the crap scared out of him. Brooding on his misfortunes he hunkered down into the saddle and settled for a long, chilly ride.

CHAPTER TWELVE

As he rode through the sage-scented night under the cold, winking stars Harvey began to appreciate he needed to create a diversion, or, better still, lose his trail altogether in the wild places, for there was sure to be a posse on his back-trail. But he figured he had one ace in the hole: they wouldn't know which direction he took when he left town and that would give him time. But he would not take chances.

His best bet would be to reach the Snake Back country before dawn broke. Even if the posse guessed right and got on his trail he could still lose them in that jumble of canyons. Once that was accomplished he could back-trail, swing across the castellated faces of the Snake Backs, enter the High Tips and head for Garford Creek.

He was thinking more clearly now.

He needed to know in whose name the fifty-thousand dollars was deposited, and he was now bitterly regretful he didn't take the trouble to find out when he had the chance, for he felt sure knowing it would have perhaps led him to the killer.

Harvey rubbed his bristled chin. He knew he was playing a hunch thinking that, but his instincts had served him well of late.

There would be a posse, of course – he harboured no doubts about that – and most likely Abe Latter would be heading it. According to his pa the Turlock deputy could read sign like a native. Another thing needed to be to be considered, too: he needed water, food and ammunition. Well, he could get those things off Grover Ash at Eagle Bluff waystation.

A coyote was yipping out on the flats, a lonely, wistful sound that held his attention for a moment before he steered his mind back to his thoughts. There was another alternative: he could head for the Crossed R. But he wiped that out of his thinking immediately. He didn't want to bring his troubles down on Slim Pickett, or Sarah. He was sure they would not agree with his decision not to contact them but there was a good reason for that: more than likely the ranch would be the first place the posse would head for.

The night cold began to eat into him. His body freckled with goosepimples and he beat his hands and blew into them and pulled his denim range-coat tighter about him. But still riven with conjecture and finding no meaningful answers, he progressed across the flats. Close on midnight a half-moon lifted above the eastern hills. Despite the fact he was familiar with this dry country, and the star-shine he was using to light his trail was adequate, he was nevertheless grateful for this extra luminescence and began to make even better progress.

By the time he reached the Snake Backs the rising sun was blushing the red rock to a rosy salmon pink. On a better day he would relish the sight. But on this day he was mourning the death of his surrogate father – a man he respected above all other men – and he was in the middle of a mystery he could not make head nor tail of.

It was deeply frustrating. He was not used to uncertainty. He was used to dissembling a problem, finding a solution and then seeing it through.

Now entering the canyon country he headed for Indian Tanks – the little-known holes of seep water in the cap rock. They seldom ran dry, no matter how long a drought lasted.

Along with the gelding he drank deeply.

His thirst satisfied, he filled his canteens and then gazed speculatively at the fantasy of red rock chasms and ramparts stretching away all around him.

It was a wondrous sight for sure.

Most of the canyons were still in deep shade. Dark clumps of ponderosa stood proud on shelves jutting out from the almost sheer cliffs. Some aspen, sycamore and pine covered other ledges and slopes.

The aspens shimmered in the early light as breezes stirred them.

Not a glimmer of human life was to be seen, but birdsong filled the air and deer and mountain goats – specks in the distance – cropped the grasses growing on the narrow glades and on the ridges. But he was not comforted by such tranquillity. Most likely early-rising sourdoughs would be panning the creeks that flowed through those deep places. More often than not they were sharp-eyed, capable and inquisitive men, even though some of them became a little crazy due to the loneliness of their lives and the harsh conditions they faced.

Harvey narrowed his eyes. Yeah, his first priority must be to avoid humankind. He must make things as difficult as possible for the posse, who could certainly be asking questions of those reclusive men, should they meet up with them. But one thing was in his favour: most hard rock mining was done in the wild places further west. Maybe a hundred men – maybe a lot more – laboured on those sites and he would almost certainly be seen by at least one or more of them, should he head that way.

Half an hour on, false trail laid, he turned the gelding south and cut across the faces of the Snake Backs then swung north towards the foothills of the High Tip Range. An hour later and sweating in the now rapidly rising temperature he eased the gelding up an Indian trail he knew into the cooler foothills.

For moments – pausing on a ridge – he allowed his gaze to search the flats below, fading away to the south, into distant silver haze. He couldn't see any dust that would suggest a posse in pursuit. The only movement he saw was a speck in the far distance. It must be the seven o'clock stage out of Turlock, rocking along the Garford Creek road. A long train of dust was hanging in the still air behind it. It was clearly heading for Coronado Sinks waystation to change horses and slake his thirst and take a breather.

There was no other sign of activity.

At Shadow Creek, half a mile up from the

ambush site, he topped up his canteens and let his sweat-flecked gelding drink sparingly. After that he groomed the beast and let it rest and graze on the lush grass before turning to his own needs. He stripped and dived into the deep pool below the waterfall he stopped by and washed the grime and tiredness off and out of him.

Half an hour later he mounted again and headed across the stream. He followed the stage road into the main body of the High Tips. But he didn't use the trail for long and turned off into the higher country. An hour later, from a high ridge, he watched the Turlock-Garford Creek stage sway and rock through one of the narrow passes far below, heading for the Eagle Bluff waystation.

The sight gave him some satisfaction. For sure, the Trans-Mountain Coach Company should be congratulated for pioneering such a good passageway through this formidable mountain range. A lot of dynamite must have been used to make it so. Perhaps one day they would push the railroad through and that would open up a lot of things. And, on further speculation, if the gold strike proved to be a bonanza, maybe the railroad would come sooner than anyone anticipated. But seeing the coach made him realize he would have to wait until the stage went through Eagle bluff before he could use the various services Grover Ash provided.

He found shelter in the trees and put the gelding on a long rope and allowed it to graze once more.

The cool of the shade was heaven.

An hour after noon he reined up before the stage post's main building. A man of long acquaintance, Grover Ash welcomed him cordially. Grover was a tall, thin black man with a sad brown gaze. As usual, the Chiricahua Apache youth, Achay, who helped Grover with the horses and other chores around the place, was hovering near the open barn doors. The Indian stared at him with dark, sombre eyes before nodding acknowledgement and continuing his work. Achay would speak and socialize only when he felt he needed to. Harvey always figured he was on good terms with the youth, but you could never tell with an Apache.

As for Grover Ash: he and Grant Watson always got on fine, went back a long way. Grover was shipped out with the Fifth Cavalry to help deal with the Indian troubles a couple of years after the peace was signed at Appomattox Courthouse. When Grover finished his service thirteen years later, he decided to stay on in the territory. With his army savings he set up the waystation and made it work. The Trans-Mountain Coach Company willingly paid him a fee to use his services, to save them the hassle of maintaining such an out-of-way place.

Now in the cool of the main building and seated at the long table specifically there for stage customers to eat their meal at, Grover Ash expressed his sadness upon hearing about Harvey's father's death. He said he picked the news up from yesterday's stage driver.

Harvey now ate the buck stew provided while Ash busied himself gathering the trail victuals he required. He also bought powder, shot and caps for his Colt Army and the Dragoon pistol.

'Yo' for business, sah?' Ash said.

'You could say that.'

'That's good to hear. Your pa, he was a fine man.'

The 'sah', Harvey detested. He was 'Harve' to his friends. But Grover insisted upon it. He said it was hard to break the habits of a lifetime. There was also the whip scars on his back to suggest the 'habit' was driven into him.

Harvey moved outside and busied himself loading his victuals. When he turned from his chores Grover was standing watching him from the stoop.

He said, 'I haven't been here, Grover. You understand me?'

He pressed notes into the black man's horny hand. Ash looked down at the money and looked hurt. 'No need for this, sah. I know how to keep ma tongue still, especially where ma friends are concerned.'

'Take it anyway,' Harvey said. 'Call it a gift.' Then he fumbled in his vest pocket and brought out a silver dollar. 'Pass this on to Achay.'

Ash grinned wisely. 'Yes, sah, but he'll bite it first, that Apache. He don't trust anybody 'cept maybe me. But I sometimes git doubts about that belief! Real close native, that Achay.'

Harvey climbed into the saddle, touched the brim of his sweat-stained hat. 'Always a pleasure visiting with you, Grover.'

Ash's ready smile broadened. 'Likewise with you, sah,' he said. 'Will you be calling agin later, when you done the business?'

'It is my intention. I'm still down on my poker winnings. You play a mean game, Mr Ash.'

'But a fair one, sah,' said Grover.

'I'll give you that.'

Harvey turned the gelding and touched its flanks lightly with his heels.

Out of sight of the waystation Harvey once more turned the steel-grey off the stage road and trailed into the mountains. Here he made another diversion – always mindful that a posse may be behind him – and headed south this time, as though he was returning to the Sontan Basin.

A mile into the High Tips, a hard trail to follow once again laid, he swung the gelding north, towards Garford Creek.

As he rode he fingered his pa's law badge, taken off his pa's vest at the death scene and now kept in the right pocket of his two-pocket vest. Grim, hard lines set a look beyond his years across his young face. 'One thing is for sure, Pa, I'll get him,' he said. 'If it takes me ten years, by God I'll get him.'

CHAPTER THIRTEEN

Noon, a day on, Harvey rode up to the multi tie-rail in front of the Rest A Spell Saloon in the heart of bustling Garford Creek. Before he entered the town he bathed in the stream a mile out, beyond the settlement, then boiled water, shaved and generally cleaned up. He figured a visit to the bank would require him to be as presentable as possible. After so many days riding with little respite he was sure he looked nothing other than a saddle tramp. As for his fears regarding Latter or Tate being here with a posse ... up to now he had seen no evidence of either. But that wasn't to say they wouldn't be here. He just hadn't clapped eyes on them.

At the Rest A Spell he drank two cold beers and then headed for the Contention Livery Barn on Ashmole Street. There he asked for his tired steel-grey to be grained, groomed and temporarily stalled before he headed for Garford Creek City Bank. Arriving at the bank, a quiet word with the teller at the first grille he came to soon got him in to see the bank manager, who, as he already knew, was a well-dressed, urbane man greying at the temples. However, when he entered the office the fellow didn't seem to recognize him, which Harvey found unusual considering the large amount of money he deposited there not too long ago.

In the privacy of his office the manager sat down behind his polished desk, motioned for Harvey to sit in the chair on the other side. Then he eyed him carefully before he smiled professionally and said, 'So, what can we do for you, er, sir?'

Harvey flashed his pa's badge. 'I'm Sheriff Grant Watson, out of Turlock. I need some information regarding the payment of fifty-thousand dollars I made here recently.'

'Ah, yes,' said the manager, enlightenment flooding into his bland features. 'I thought I recognized your face. Yes, a very large sum indeed. Hmm, what kind of information do you require, Sheriff?'

'In whose name was the sum deposited?'

The bank manager looked surprised he was even being asked the question. 'I'm afraid I cannot divulge such private information, Sheriff Watson,' he said courteously. 'Indeed, it is most definitely against the bank's policy. The identity of our customers, you must appreciate, needs to be protected at all times.'

Harvey tried to remain calm. If, as he pessimistically assumed, the posse was in town, he didn't have time to debate finer points. He needed to get what he wanted and get out. He said, 'I accept that need under normal circumstances, but one man has been killed and another severely injured because of that money. Now, that tends to put a different complexion on things, wouldn't you say?'

Still the bank manager didn't seem inclined to accommodate him. Instead, he sighed and smiled indulgently. 'Sheriff Watson, of course it is the policy of the bank to help the law in any way we can. But, I can only reiterate, the bank does have rules – obligations if you like – regarding the identity of its customers and I am duty-bound to abide by them. I'm sorry, but that's the way it is.'

Slow anger was building up in Harvey. His pa was dead. Lucas Skinner was shot up and gravely ill. He was wrongly accused of attempted murder and on the run. On top of that he was saddle-sore and extremely frustrated by this man's evasions. His stare was bleak as it riveted on the fellow the other side of the desk. He said, 'I'll give you ten seconds, mister, then, if a name is not forthcoming, I'll tear this office apart piece

133

by piece until I find the file that tells it. Now, d'you understand me?'

The manager's rosy complexion paled. 'Really, sir, are you threatening me?' He began fidgeting with a neat, small pile of papers on his desk as if retidying them. 'This is most irregular – most irregular. Indeed, not the conduct I would expect from an officer of the law, I must say.'

Harvey brought his right fist crashing down on the desktop making everything upon it bounce.

'Get me the name, dammit!'

The force of Harvey's words brought the manager up from his seat, alarm flaring across his well-fed face.

'Well, really. I can only do this under protest.'

Haughtily, he crossed to the three grey filing-cabinets standing against the back wall, near the window. He opened the top drawer of the middle one and took out a thin folder. He came back to the desk and offered it. 'Rest assured,' he said with a tilt of his chin, 'I will be making the strongest possible complaint to all the relevant authorities.'

Harvey was already scanning the papers.

'Do that,' he said, not even bothering to look at the man.

He read the file. The name within stunned him. He handed it back. 'I thank you for your time.' He touched the brim of his hat. 'I'll let myself out.'

When he stepped outside he walked up Main, keeping in the shadows. At the Majestic Hotel – a boarding-house down a side street on the north edge of town he used whenever he was here – he booked a room.

The grand name didn't fit the basic amenities offered there, but it was reasonably clean and the proprietor was discreet, if asked to be. Harvey now decided that if there was a posse in town it was more than a probability they would have made their presence known by now. They hadn't done, so he felt he could confidently risk grabbing a few hours' sleep before heading for ... where? To the person in whose name the fifty thousand was put? It didn't need thinking about. That person must be the leak, or the person who ordered his death. But then, no way could he bring himself to believe that either.

He reached his room and shut the door behind him. He undressed and drew the drab curtains to shut out the strong sun before flopping down on the ironframe bed. Sleep came almost immediately.

CHAPTER FOURTEEN

Harvey became aware of the metallic clicks of a Colt coming to full cock. Cold, intense fear crawled across his gut.

He opened his eyes.

Using what little light there was in the curtain-darkened room he stared into the bore of a long barrelled Colt .45, not three feet from his nose. The man sitting on the edge of the bed behind it displayed a marshal's badge on his grey vest. A Volcanic rifle, Harvey saw, was grasped in his bony left hand.

Marshal Jake Neilson said, 'What in the hell d' you think you're doing, Harve, booking in here? You gone *loco*, or something?'

Harvey looked into the lawman's craggy face. Jake Neilson was Garford Creek's law and a longtime friend of both he and his pa. On top of that Jake was a common-sense badge man and as good as they come. Despite that, this was going to be an interesting few minutes.

He said, 'Is there a Turlock posse in town?'

'They ain't called on me if there is,' said Neilson.

Harvey raised his brows and made a gesture with his hand. 'Well, to answer your question, I was plain plumb-tuckered out, Jake. And I half figured you'd give me a break when you got to know I was in town. I guess the bank manager let you know, uh?'

Neilson straightened, looked severe. 'You figured he wouldn't? You scared the shit out of one of the town's most influential men. On top of that you posed as your pa, for God's sake. *On top of that*, don't you know you're posted wanted throughout the whole territory for attempted murder?'

'The word's out, uh?' Harvey said.

'You'd better believe it,' Neilsen said. He decocked the Colt and slid it into the well-used holster on his right hip. 'Now, what's your story, son?'

Harvey told it, leaving nothing out. Finishing, he looked at the lawman. 'Give me half an hour to get clear of town, Jake. That's all I ask.'

Neilson screwed up his leathery face, making it clear he didn't like being imposed upon in this way. *'All?'* he said. 'I'm the law here, boy, and you're accused of attempted murder. How do I know that accusation ain't true?'

'You know it isn't,' Harvey said.

Neilson scowled. 'I know nothing, only what has come out of the law office at Turlock and what you say. If I'm going to do my job I should put friendships aside, take you in and let the law take its course.'

Harvey eased himself tiredly off the bed and began dressing.

'Half an hour, Jake,' he said.

Neilson glowered. 'Damnmit, Harve, I'm a lawman,' he said. 'You know what the law meant to your pa?'

'Sure I do.'

'Well, it means the same to me, dammit.'

Harvey said, 'I respect that. But Pa also said a man needed to use a little discretion now and again.'

'Meaning I won't?'

Clearly irritated, Neilson began pacing the room. 'Dammit, boy, you don't know what you're asking me to do.' He stopped pacing and sighed heavily. 'Look, let me run what you said past you, before I make my decision. Some Mexican ambushed you in the High Tips. You plugged him. Before he died you questioned him, but got nothing out of him. Then your pa got gunned down. After that, an assailant shot this fellow, Lucas Skinner, but they pinned the shooting on you.'

Harvey nodded. 'You got it, but I figure the bullet that hit Skinner had my name written on it.'

'Because somebody got to know about the money and hired the greaser to kill and rob you?' Neilson said.

'Yeah.'

'But you swung it around and killed him?'

'That's right.'

'But you reckon this mystery person now thinks the Mexican spilled the beans before he died and he wants your hide?'

Harvey nodded. 'In a nutshell.'

Neilson was now rubbing his deeply cleft jaw. 'Dammit, boy,' he said. 'You're putting me in a bad position here.'

'I didn't do it, Jake,' Harvey said. 'And, if I'm to have any chance of finding Pa's killer, I've got to keep out of the calaboose.'

'Hell, you think I don't know that?'

Marshal Neilson was clearly torn right down the middle. 'Dammit, Harve,' he said again. 'This isn't fair!'

'Pa's murder wasn't fair, Jake.'

Neilson glared, his face reddening. 'That's below the belt, boy, and I won't have it.' He sighed and fastened his iron-grey gaze on to Harvey's. 'Look, Jervis Freeman, the bank manager, knows I came for you and he has real power in this town. Dammit, I could lose my job if he figures out I let you go.'

'I was gone before you got here,' Harvey said.

Neilson snorted. 'That easy, uh? Well, Fred Berry, the owner of this establishment, knows you weren't.'

'Talk to him,' said Harvey. 'He'll listen. He knows me.' While he talked he finished dressing.

Neilson was now clearly worrying on his problem. He didn't even look as Harvey pushed Shorty Tate's fully loaded Colt Dragoon into his waist-belt and placed the Colt Army into his gun holster.

Neilson sighed heavily. 'OK, we'll play it this way, son. You get the advantage of me. You tie me up.'

A huge burden seemed to lift off Harvey's shoulders. The idea of having to draw on his old friend – and his pa's – was troubling him, but he would have done it if the need arose. He only hoped Jake didn't try to stop him if it came to that.

'I'm indebted,' he said.

Neilson took his arm in a grip of steel, his stare penetrating. 'Just get your pa's killer, boy,' he said.

Harvey nodded sombrely. 'If it's the last thing I do.'

He got to work. He tore the sheet on the bed into strips, bound the marshal's arms and legs and then gagged him. Then he stared at Neilson's Volcanic rifle, now leaned against the scarred dresser. Man, that would be useful. He picked it up. The marshal mumbled angrily behind his gag, glared, clearly objecting to him taking it.

'I'll make sure you get it back, Jake,' Harvey said.

More irate protests came but Harvey ignored them and stepped over to the door. He took a deep breath and opened it then peered up and down the long landing. It was like a dark tunnel illuminated by one oil lamp. It was deserted. He knew at the opposite end of the landing from the stairs leading to the lounge there was a door that led out to the outside back stairs.

He moved briskly towards it. Once outside he set his hat to shade his face. He took the stairs casually, hoping not to raise curious stares. Once in the back alley he headed for the Contention Livery Barn. Entering the long stable-building he briskly walked down the runway to the gelding's stall. The handsome animal greeted him warmly.

After briefly petting it, Harvey saddled up, mounted and trotted it out on to the back lot. The stable attendant, he saw, was busy at the manure stacks. As he passed him the hostler gave him a wave and Harvey flipped a salute back.

'See you again, fella?' the hostler called.

'Reckon it's likely.'

There was no need to stop. Stabling fees were paid up.

Once out on the grassy flat country before the High Tip Mountains Harvey put the gelding into a canter and headed for the soaring, white-topped peaks.

CHAPTER FIFTEEN

As Harvey headed towards the mountains all sorts of ideas began running through his mind, some ludicrous, some making sense. But first priority, he figured, he needed to have words with the owner of the fifty-thousand dollars, though he was still staggered by the name revealed.

He took a little-known Indian trail into the mountains and headed for Sontan Basin.

He still wasn't sure there was no pursuit and decided evasion still held high priority in his book of do's and don'ts.

He gazed at the cobalt-blue sky. The late afternoon sun was already starting to cast long shadows. But the gelding was causing him worries. Already it was beginning to flag. He decided it wasn't surprising, the amount of work it had put in over the past week or so. Indeed, even he was beginning to feel the strain: aching back and legs, general stiffness. He could handle it. Being a cowman often meant long hours in the saddle, especially during roundup and trail drives. But the horses the boys rode during those times weren't usually run into the ground; they were changed frequently. Like most big outfits the Crossed R ran a large remuda. He decided, out of respect for the horse, that once he got into the mountains he would make early camp. There were still victuals left, plus oats for the animal. And another day wasn't going to make a deal of difference now. He continued to climb.

An hour later, breaking out of the pines and topping a long ridge, he looked back. In the far distance the undulating grass plain between the mountains and Garford Creek was tranquil. Colours were varying from deep purple to red, orange and yellow in the setting sun.

There was no hint of a posse – maybe Marshal Neilson had not been discovered yet? All he could see were a couple of wagons and a lone rider heading across country, no doubt heading for their home ranch.

He began to relax and look for a campsite. But, startling him, lead ripped through his hat and sent it down the steep side of the ridge to lodge amongst the rocks and brush fifty feet below. The booming rifle that caused the mayhem sent flat echoes into the mountains, repeating into near infinity.

Anxiety bunched into Harvey's throat as he dragged Jake Neilson's Volcanic out of its scabbard and went out of the saddle and into the cover of the rocks nearby. Snorting its fright, the gelding raced down the slope into the trees.

Silence.

Harvey crouched in the undergrowth amongst the rocks, his ears straining to pick up any sound. All the time his mind was working, seeking countermeasures. He felt for small rocks. He could toss them and did. They rattled into the bushes.

No reaction, but there was distance between him and the bushwhacker. Maybe

144

the noise went unnoticed.

He licked his lips and stared at the wooded rise above the rocky ridge he was on. A swift appraisal of what went before suggested the shot came from there. Then he saw it, the slight movement of grass between some low-growing junipers on the outer fringes of the rocks lining the upper reaches of the ridge above the trees.

Got you!

Suppressing his excitement he levered off three shots. A jackrabbit leapt out of the grass and high into the air, clearly in its death throes, half its head shot away.

Jesus!

Lead began screaming down off the ridge, ripping into the ground around him with soapy thuds. Fear rampaged through him. He rolled desperately. More bullets dug up spouts of soil, but he kept rolling down the ridge until he crashed into the sprawl of aspens a quarter of the way down.

He scrambled into their safety.

Winded by the impact of hitting the trees, his heart thumping like a trip-hammer against his ribs, he still expected lead to zap into him the moment he exposed himself to return fire. But he needed to try and did. More bullets savaged lumps out of the tree bole he was crouching behind.

Raw fury ran through him. Damn, that was enough! He drew Neilson's Volcanic into his shoulder and levered off three rapid shots and to hell with it.

His lead snarled and ripped amongst the rocks up there. Then, once more, came the eternal quiet of the mountains.

He wiped his sweaty lips with the back of his hairy hand and gripped the wood and metal of his warm rifle.

What next?

It came as a complete surprise to see horse and rider breaking out of the trees up there, heading for the Turlock-Garford Creek trail far, far below. The rider was too far away to be recognized. Nevertheless, Harvey reared up and jacked off two shots but failed to make a hit. Soon the rider was lost amongst the stands of trees. Two minutes later he came out on to open parkland lower down.

Harvey could only stare helplessly after him.

CHAPTER SIXTEEN

It took Harvey fifteen minutes to round up his horse, despite repeated whistles. He put it into a gallop after the bushwhacker, who was now barely a speck in the distance and heading for Garford Creek. By the time Harvey entered the town it was dark and he figured he was twenty minutes behind the ambusher.

Deep frustration filled him for all he had to go on was the colour of the bushwhacker's horse, a red roan as far as he could make out.

Passing the tie rails lining Main, he used what lamp illumination there was to try and pick out the horse. It was a slim chance because that colour of roan was common. His only hope was to look for a badly lathered animal, but he drew a blank there, too. Now, the heat and fervour of the chase subsiding, he realized he was placed firmly back in the pickle barrel, riding into town like this. What was more, he was putting Jake Neilson in an impossible position, should he be caught. It was unfair to once more depend

147

on the marshal's friendship to bail him out.

To attempt to fade into the background he mixed in with riders on the streets. Being cattle country, range men were the predominant group and being a cowman himself it was easy to blend in.

He passed the marshal's office. He was surprised to see Neilson was sitting at his desk, apparently writing up his daybook using the small ring of light from an oil lamp. The rest of the office, Harvey observed, was in virtual darkness.

He guessed there could be a hell of a lot going into that book and none of it in his favour. But why wasn't there any pursuit? Perhaps Jake Neilson didn't think the incident at the bank merited a chase? That didn't hold water either. Harvey Munson was still wanted for attempted murder, any way you looked at it. And where was the Turlock posse? But if he could nail the owner of that roan, things might look up. And Jake Neilson, being a lawman, must be an astute observer of all things suspicious, particularly if it was entering his town. Harvey rubbed his chin. So maybe Jake spotted the rider who took those potshots at him in the mountains when he came chasing into town not so long ago? It was a possibility. And going on what his pa often reminisced about Jake Neilson ... that craggy lawman didn't miss much.

Harvey set his jaw into a grim line.

He needed to take another chance.

He guided his horse down the narrow alley beside the law office. He knew there was a door that led into the cellblock at the back. He reined up at the tie-ring hanging from the brick wall by the cellblock, dismounted and tied up. Surprisingly, the door was unlocked. He eased his way in, hardly daring to breathe and closed the door. A single lantern was burning on a ledge set into the wall. A prisoner was snoring loudly in one of the three cells. The rest of the cells, Harvey observed, were empty.

He went up the passageway leading to the office. Entering it, he saw Jake Neilson was still bent over, busily writing. The pale yellow light from the single lamp in the desk didn't reach the corners of the office, leaving them in near darkness.

'Howdy, Jake,' he said.

Neilson swung round his swivel chair, his surprise plain. Then he growled, 'Dammit, Harve, I thought you'd be long gone.'

'Got interrupted, shot at in the mountains. You see a rider come hell-for-leather into town just now aboard a red roan?'

Neilson frowned. 'Can't say I did. You say you been shot at again?'

'Yeah,' said Harvey. 'A lone rifleman – him on the damned roan. Couldn't have been a posse.'

Neilson smiled. 'Well, I can relieve your feelings there, son. There's no posse on your trail – you've been cleared.'

Harvey narrowed his eyelids. 'What d'you mean?'

Abe Latter's voice came from behind him. 'Skinner came to, Harve – vouched you had nothing to do with the shooting.'

Harvey spun on his heel. The Turlock deputy was sitting in the gloom of the far right corner. He was smiling.

Not knowing whether to laugh or cry, Harvey said, 'Well, I'll be damned.' Then he squinted. 'How about Shorty Tate?'

Latter pursed his lips. 'Goes without saying he ain't pleased you whacked him, but he's been advised to forget it.'

Harvey frowned. 'By whom?'

Latter rose from the chair and came into the light. 'By me,' he said. 'I've been made acting sheriff until elections can be organized.'

Harvey felt genuine warmth fill him. He liked Latter. He offered his hand, which the deputy took, equally as amiably.

'Couldn't have happened to a better man,' Harvey said. 'I'm real pleased for you, Abe.' Then he frowned, as if mystified. 'But, damn, you didn't come all this way just to break *that* news. You could have used the telegraph.'

Latter nodded. 'True. Had to bring a prisoner in to catch the three o'clock southbound. US Marshals were waiting here to collect him, so I killed two birds with one stone. Just called in the office to chew a little fat – trade information if you like – with Jake before I headed back to Turlock.'

Harvey frowned. 'Tonight?'

'Figure I need to,' said Latter, 'Shorty being on his own. Got to be a real wild town on our hands back there.'

'I guess so,' said Harvey. 'Got anything to point towards Pa's killer yet?'

Latter shook his head. 'Nothing. But we'll get him, don't you fret.'

'I'll be joining you soon as I get back to town. You got objections?'

'No. Fact is, consider yourself deputized right now. Jake will be witness. You riding back with me?'

Harvey felt a strong urge to do so but he badly needed rest, more so his horse. But he felt a little guilt, as well as frustration. He should be getting after his pa's killer. But Abe was a good lawman; he would be doing his best and he would be joining him soon.

'Guess I'll pass,' he said. 'My hoss needs rest.'

Latter grinned. 'Being on the run ain't much fun, uh?'

Harvey nodded and smiled along with the acting sheriff.

'You'd better believe it.'

Just then Jake Neilson said, 'You're welcome to stay the night with us, Harve. Jane will soon fit you up with a bed and she'll be tickled pink to lay out another plate, especially for you.' Jane was Jake's wife.

Harvey said, 'It'll be good to talk with you all again. It's been too long.'

'So it's done,' said Neilson, his pleasure clearly apparent.

Latter groaned. 'Some fellows have all the luck,' He extended a hand to Jake Neilson and Neilson took it. 'Always a pleasure talking with you, Jake,' Latter said.

'And you,' Neilson said. 'Take care through those mountains.'

Latter drew himself up to his full six feet and sighed. 'Sure. Well, I guess I need to be getting along.' He turned for the door. 'Have a good evening, gents. I envy you.'

Harvey and Neilson watched him go then Harvey said, 'So how about that supper? I'm starving.'

'When I get my Volcanic back,' said Jake.

Harvey pulled a face. 'You got a Winchester I can borrow?'

Neilson nodded to the gun rack. Harvey saw there was a Winchester and two shotguns propped in it.

'Take the Winchester, but return it. Got to account for it come spring audit.'

Harvey grinned. 'Don't you trust me?'

Neilson grinned and patted him on the back. 'Whatever gave you that idea?'

Harvey reached for the long gun.

CHAPTER SEVENTEEN

Five o'clock the following morning Harvey rode out of Garford Creek. The town basked quietly in the dawn's golden sunrise. The streets he rode through were deserted. Sixteen miles out, at Dawson Gap waystation, he turned the gelding off the mountain road and took the Indian trail through the High Tips.

At nine o'clock with the night starlit, he descended onto the Turlock-Garford Creek road, a mile north of Eagle Bluff waystation.

He was looking forward to supper and a few hands of cards with Grover Ash before climbing into one of Grover's bunks to enjoy a good night's sleep but the slight rustle, trail-side, put every nerve on alert.

Achay, Grover's Indian worker, materialized out of the shadows of the pines. Squat, dark and sombre-faced the boy stood before him on the dark road.

Harvey allowed himself to relax and decocked the Colt Dragoon he drew as soon as he heard the noise. But he could not avoid growling, 'Dammit, boy, I could have killed you.'

'But Munson didn't,' said the Apache. 'Achay know who he can trust.'

Then, unusually – for Achay was usually so impassive – Achay's face showed serious concern.

'Ash in trouble, Munson,' he said. 'You come with Achay now.'

Sure he wasn't hearing right – what enemies did Grover Ash have? – Harvey held up a hand. 'Hold it. You'd better explain yourself a little better, fella.'

Achay shuffled impatiently – again unusual

154

because Harvey knew from experience patience was one of the Native American's biggest assets. They'd wait out eternity if they had to.

Achay said, 'Two men come. They want Ash to stay quiet when you reach station. I was in barn, like usual. They not know about me. I creep up to window. I see one man was beating Ash.'

Stunned by the news Harvey narrowed his eyelids and said, hoarsely, 'D'you know who they are?'

'One is El Lobo,' said Achay.

'*El Lobo?*'

'Very bad *hombre*,' said Achay. 'They say they want Munson. They say they kill you when you come. They say they know you are coming. El Zorro, the other one, he not sure about killing you, though.'

'*El Zorro?*'

What the hell was going on?

'Both very bad *hombres*,' Achay was saying. 'Knew them in Mexico. They kill my mother and father and grandfather to sell their scalps.'

A chill now sprinkled up Harvey's backbone. He knew about that barbaric practice – scalp hunting for money.

'The hell they did,' he said.

Achay nodded. 'I was boy. We were in the Sierra Madres, near Geronimo's camp. Big Nose Captain – Lieutenant Charles Gatewood – and his Apache scouts were looking for Geronimo. Found Geronimo hiding out in canyon. Geronimo surrendered along with Naiche and some others. My mother and father and my grandfather ran away. We tried to get to stronghold where we would be safe but El Lobo and his *bandidos* found us. Like I said, they killed my family to sell their scalps to the Mexicans. My mother threw me in bushes so I escaped. Later I was caught and taken to white man's school. Two snows later I escaped from there, too, after I learned white man's talk.'

Harvey now felt the rest of Achay's history, chilling yet interesting though it was, could wait until a better time.

He said, 'Was Ash still alive when you left?'

'Yes. I think they keep him alive for something.'

'I'm inclined to go along with that.' Harvey looked soberly at Achay. 'You've done well, boy.'

Achay grunted, his usually passive face showing what could be construed as satisfaction. Harvey urged the gelding forward and Achay fell in beside him, jogging easily.

Munson knew the Apache could keep up this sort of pace all day. And Achay, being Chiricahua, with the same blood as Mangas Colorado and Cochise running through his veins, would also be a formidable opponent, despite his youth. Apache boys, he knew, were trained to be killers from an early age.

A hundred yards from the waystation – a large dark adobe oblong framed against the starlit sky – Harvey eased the gelding to a stop. Yellow light shone out of the only window in front of the building.

All appeared normal.

Of course it did.

He turned to Achay, who had hardly broken sweat.

'Where are their horses, Achay?'

'They put them in barn, to hide, but left saddles on.' The youth pushed out his chest. 'I unsaddle them and take them outside and let them go.'

Harvey nodded.

But now came the dilemma, as well as the terrible truths. He didn't know whether Ash was alive or dead. Further, he didn't know why Ash had been captured and why he was abused and asked to keep quiet. It must have something to do with all that had gone on lately and it could only be Harvey Mun-

157

son the scum were interested in.

But the names El Lobo and El Zorro were meaningless. Mexicans? Where did they fit into his life? He had never heard of them. Could they be friends of the bastard he killed in the High Tip foothills and were now seeking revenge?

He turned. 'Achay.' He lifted out the Colt Army from the holster on his right hip and handed it to the boy. 'You know how to use one of these?'

The Apache boy looked at him gravely.

'I know.'

Harvey nodded. 'Good. Now, I want you to go out the back of the station and wait. Stop anybody who tries to get to the horses. Can you do that?'

Achay swelled out his chest once more. 'Achay warrior, kill two Mexicans. Maybe now kill El Lobo and El Zorro, uh?'

Before Munson could reply, to tell the boy not to make any stupid moves, the Chiricahua youth melted into the night.

Harvey waited a few moments and then mounted and trotted the gelding the last hundred yards or so to the waystation. He did it as nonchalantly as he could. He wanted to keep everything looking normal, play along. But in truth he was wound up as taut as stretched catgut. He didn't know what to expect.

The waystation, he saw, was still lit up. Bound to be, he decided, if he was meant to walk right into an ambush.

At the tie rail he dismounted and called, 'Hey, Grover, get the God-damned stew on the table and loosen up those pasteboards while I put up my horse, uh?'

The night silence seemed to stretch to infinity then an anguished shout. 'Get out of here, Harvey. It's a tra–'

A gun roared. There was a cry.

Expecting something, but not that, Harvey reacted unusually – that is, directly. Feeling as though his gut was hitting the back of his throat and fearing for Grover's life he ran up the two steps on to the ramada. He hammered on the door as if he were going to break it in, and then moved swiftly to the right, to the one large window.

A raging volley of lead punched holes through the door, ripping out large splinters of wood, sending them flying into the night.

Staring through the window Harvey made a hasty perusal, instantly taking in the whole of the waystation's interior.

Crouched behind the small bar against the far wall he saw Shorty Tate blazing away at the door with his Smith and Wesson Russian plus a Colt .45, held in his left hand. Grover Ash, Harvey saw, was tied to a chair in the centre of the room and slumped over. He looked in a bad way.

Gritting his teeth Harvey brought up the Dragoon and fired. Tate immediately yelled and his beefy features registered complete surprise as he was flung back by the impact of the big Dragoon's lead. He was staring at the window as he crashed against the back wall of the waystation before rebounding forward. His head came down hitting the bar top with a bone jarring thump. Blood, Harvey saw, was pumping out of the two wounds he made where Tate's heart should be. Then, as helpless as a puppet whose strings were cut, Shorty Tate slithered down behind the bar. Harvey held no doubt the vicious Turlock deputy was dead before he hit the board floor.

He made for the door, to give aid to Grover Ash, but a shrieking cry from the back of the waystation brought him to a halt. Achay? Had the other son of a bitch got the boy? Further to that: what about his good friend Ash?

'Grover, you all right?' he called anxiously. There was a grunt, then, 'I's keep for now, sah. Go see 'bout the boy.'

Harvey took Ash's word for it. The man was a seasoned campaigner.

He raced to the rear of the station. Under the light of the stars he was relieved to see Achay was standing over a writhing figure. He saw the Apache's big Bowie – which he always carried – was shaping up to take the man's topknot. The Colt, apparently, was forgotten.

'Achay,' Harvey shouted, 'that is not the way of your people!'

Achay paused, turned, his face a savage mask. 'White man take Apache scalp for money. What is wrong with Apache taking white man's scalp?'

'You want to be like the white man?'

Achay's Bowie remained poised for some moments – clearly the words made an impact on him – then he flung the man away from him.

'Achay no want to be like white man. Is Ash OK?'

Harvey nodded. 'Go to him. I figure he could use help. I'll deal with this.'

Achay sheathed the knife and without another word went past him into the way-station. Harvey moved to the moaning figure, lying prone on the ground. Using the starlight he stared into the face of Abe Latter.

'Abe ... what the hell?'

Latter was clutching his bloody stomach, as if he was trying to prevent the contents of it spilling out. He gasped, 'Damned Apache gutted me. Came out of nowhere.'

Anger flooded through Harvey. Just what the hell was going on here?

'You'd better start talking, Abe,' he said.

'Shorty – he dead?' said Latter.

'Yes.'

Latter groaned, his face an agony-filled, terrible grimace. After moments he said, 'I haven't much time and I owe you the truth. You've been ace with me, so has your pa. Harve, it was Tate killed the sheriff.'

'*What?*' Bright anger flared through Harvey. He made to grab Latter.

Latter waved a hand. 'Hear me out. You got to understand. Shorty's my brother. Couple of weeks ago he overheard your pa talking to some fellow about shipping fifty-thousand dollars to Garford Creek. It grabbed him right off, being an owlhoot for most of his life. However, while he was listening he made some noise – always a clumsy bastard – and your pa discovered him but trusted him and swore him to secrecy.'

That was Pa, thought Harvey.

162

Latter went on, 'I got to tell you, Harve, Shorty and me ... we weren't always lawmen. Fact is, him and me been renegades for most of our lives. I didn't like it much but he was my brother. Fact is, his lawless ways scared our ma near to death and did kill her in the end. And damn her to all eternity, on her deathbed she asked me to watch over him, stay with him, protect him. I was the oldest, see, and steadiest, but I couldn't steer him away from the owlhoot. Eventually, we got into big trouble in Mexico – so big it scared the shit out of us. Imagine that, uh, big bold badmen? Anyway, we decided to go straight. We were known on the Texas side of the border, we raided there, but our faces weren't. We forged references and were going well until Shorty overheard that conversation and how much money was involved in the shipment. The temptation was too great. Anyway, he did try to box clever. To take any suspicions away from him he brought in an old *pistolero compadre* of ours, a half-breed name of Ramos Blazer to ambush you in the High Tips and take the money.' Latter grimaced and groaned, 'Jesus.' Pain was stark in his eyes, but he recovered. He went on, 'Well, I guess you know most of the rest, except that when Blazer didn't come back with the money, Shorty rode out, thinking the 'breed had made a run for it, but found his body instead. He buried him and hid the saddle. Didn't want to leave any evidence, see? Guess you wondered why it wasn't there when you got back from Garford Creek?'

Harvey held his simmering temper. 'What else?'

'Shorty figured Blazer had talked. Figured when you came back you would be on the prod for him and you'd tell your pa. That's why Shorty shot your pa – case you had – and came looking for you.'

Harvey leaned over. He grasped the front of Latter's shirt and hauled him up, face to face.

'Damn you, why didn't you stop him?'

Latter screamed with pain.

'For God's sake, Harve!'

Harvey, in humanity, let him go but was reluctant to do so.

When Latter recovered sufficiently, he said, 'I didn't stop him because I didn't know. It was only after you left the office the night you got back that Shorty came in with the story about the ambush and the shipment of the money to Garford Creek, and what he'd done about it. And by that time, he'd shot your pa.'

'But you still played along!' raged Harvey.

'I'm not proud of it,' admitted Latter, 'but what could I do, Shorty being blood kin and all? Always had to wet-nurse him and God forgive me for it. He's a brute and a killer.'

'You any better?' said Harvey.

He felt he could beat Latter to a pulp, and cheerfully, but it was clear the deputy didn't have much longer to live and there were things he still needed to know.

'Did Shorty try to take me out and got Skinner instead?'

'Like you figured.'

Latter clasped his gut and groaned horribly. But the spasm subsided and the deputy looked up, pleading in his eyes.

'I guess sorry isn't enough, uh, Harve?'

You betcha!

'Was it you who took a shot at me in the High Tips yesterday?'

Latter nodded. 'Had this notion to frighten you, but I knew in my gut you'd never give up. But it didn't matter anyway. Shorty was waiting for me here. He'd got it all figured out – a set up. Take you out and no more worries.'

Latter now sighed and his gaze reached up. 'You know, Harve, I got to have a real liking for you and your pa, but, you got to understand, I had to go along with Shorty. Don't you see that?'

The hell I don't.

Harvey watched as the acting sheriff died, soaked in his own gore, his bloody innards hanging down over his crotch and onto the ground. Though he'd accepted Latter as a friend, Harvey now felt little for the man. He got what he deserved. But what about the gun passed through the cell window? Harvey thought. Was it part of a plot to lure him out and kill him as he made his escape? It would certainly neatly tie things up for Latter and Tate in a legal sense – shot while trying to escape. But did Latter miss with the rifle on purpose, like he claimed he did last evening in the High Tip Mountains? Harvey narrowed his eyelids. That was one thing he would never know. He turned and strode into the waystation.

Inside he found Achay was tending to Ash's wound.

As he approached Ash said, 'Before you ask, I'll live.'

Harvey felt relief and warmth fill him.

'Just one hard son of a bitch, uh, Grover?'

'Better believe it, sah.'

Achay sombrely pointed at Tate's body,

behind the bar. 'Body behind the bar is El Lobo. Him outside, he is El Zorro. I think my mother and my father and my grand-father will be happy now, uh, Munson?'

Harvey stared at the body. Tate's boots were sticking out. He saw the wolf's head logo carved into the insteps.

'Reckon they will,' he said.

Harvey knew this tragedy was over. How-ever, there was one thing still to be done. He must face the person who started all this by wanting the fifty thousand transported to Garford Creek City Bank when using the Bed Rock Bank there in Turlock would have done just as well – to his way of thinking anyway.

Any way you looked at it, this meeting was not going to be an easy one.

CHAPTER EIGHTEEN

Harvey rode easily now. The story as to what happened – and why Turlock was now light two lawmen – was told to the Turlock authorities and was believed. Grover Ash was recovering well in Ma Dugan's care, his wounds fixed by Doc Salthouse. Meantime, Achay was holding the fort at Eagle Bluff waystation.

Turlock council approached him to take care of the law in Turlock, if only temporarily. They suggested his pa must have taught him some of the ropes – which he did – but he refused the invitation. There were other fish to fry – building and running a ranch, for instance.

In the end the town council swore in John Thompson, acting on Harvey's suggestion they should approach him. John was a local man with peacekeeping experience during the seventies in the Kansas cow-towns: level-headed, handy with gun and fists and afraid of nothing. John picked Earl Forbes, the local fisticuffs champion, to act as his deputy. Earl at that moment was apprentice to George Rakes, and local blacksmith. George didn't like his trained help being poached but eventually went along with it when it was pointed out to him there were plenty of brawny boys in town seeking work. It was only a matter of training them up. They came cheaper than George, too.

While he was in town Harvey, still grieving, visited his pa's grave in the pretty town cemetery by Marsh Creek. He laid flowers.

Ma Dugan and Doc Salthouse did the burial honours in his absence and he thanked them as best he could. They refused his offer to pay for any expenses incurred. Before he left for the Crossed R he sat an hour or two with the still grieving Ma Dugan. When it came time to leave she laid a gentle hand on his arm and looked directly into his eyes.

'You'll still visit, Harvey?'

Harvey bent and kissed her lightly on the left cheek. 'Ma, wild horses won't keep me away.'

'The Lord be with you, son. That dear man would be proud of you.'

Now Harvey reined up at the tie rail before the Crossed R ranch house and dismounted. Sarah came rushing out of the house and straight into his arms and began smothering his face with kisses.

Harvey eventually extricated himself.

'Whoa, hold up, little lady.'

'We heard what happened,' Sarah blurted, 'we thought you were dead. Oh, Harvey, dear Harvey, hold me.'

Meantime Slim Pickett came down the steps, grinning fit to bust. 'It's good to have you back, son,' he said. 'The damnedest thing saying you shot down Lucas Skinner. I came into town soon as I heard, but you were gone. As for your pa ... gee, boy, I ain't got the words to express how I feel about *that*.'

Harvey looked keenly at the Crossed R owner. 'Guess we got to come to the cause of all the trouble uh, Slim ... the money I delivered to Garford Creek, the money put in Sarah's name, the money that caused all the trouble?'

Sarah gasped. '*What?* What are you talking about?'

'Ask Slim.'

The Crossed R owner turned to Sarah and waved a hand. 'Now, before you get haughty on me, girl, just you listen now.'

Sarah put her hands on her shapely hips. 'I'm listening.'

'First I got to talk to Harve.' Slim turned and Harvey met his steady grey gaze. 'Harve.' The Crossed R owner sighed heavily. 'God. I'd give a year of my life to be able to turn back the clock, but I can't. The thousand dollars I was paying out in wages for you to do the job was underhand, I admit. But your pa and I thought it was for the best seeing as you didn't want the ranch and wouldn't accept a helping hand any other way. That was why we stayed anonymous.'

'Whose idea was it?'

'It was your pa's originally,' said Slim. 'He figured you bull-headed – and I still do! – not wanting any help and suggested it was the only way to get round a stubborn cuss like you. Too obstinate for your own good were the very words he used.'

'The fifty-thousand dollars was put in Sarah's name,' said Harvey.

'Because we knew you wouldn't touch it, but women in the end are more practical,' said Slim. 'She'd know what to do when the time came.'

Sarah gasped, 'Did you say *fifty-thousand dollars!*'

Slim turned and stared at her. 'I've sold the ranch, girl, on the basis I got six months to settle my affairs. Believe me, I was going to tell you about the money before I left for Omaha.'

'Omaha!' Sarah once more put her arms akimbo. 'Dammit, I told you I can look after you!'

'D'you think so?' said Slim. 'Girl,' he waved a hand in Harvey's direction, 'you're about as stubborn as him. Running a ranch is a full-time job and I don't want to get under your feet. It was the only way I could think of to help you and Harve out in building up your ranch and all that entailed.

171

Goddammit, you two are as naïve as new-born calves if you think you can go it alone.'

'We can,' said Harvey. 'You did.'

'You *figure* you can,' snorted Slim, 'but you don't know what it takes to build up a ranch from near nothing. And you are stuck out in those mountains, with no help nearby. I had the whole of the Sontan Basin settlers to turn to if I needed it. Some day, mark my words, you're going to need a helping hand of some sort and this was the only way I could think of to give it to you.' Slim sighed and looked sad. 'But honest to God, Harve, I didn't know what delivering that money would lead to, how could I? Nor did your pa. But I'm sure he's looking down right now, happy you've come through in one piece and are ready to make your mark.'

Harvey fumbled in his mind for some suitable retaliation; could find nary a word. Truth was, looking close at it, his pa was as much a party to this as was Slim Pickett. But hell, that was easy; maybe it was *him* who was the mule-headed fool?

He felt Sarah's arm link his. 'I think it's time we moved on, Harvey,' she said. 'I reckon your pa would want that.'

He smiled down at her. 'I guess he would at that.'

She fell into his arms and he kissed her lingeringly and lovingly and thought of his ranch in the High Tips.

Watching them, contentment filled Slim Pickett's craggy features. He looked at the sky, and felt warm. 'I guess that will do for now, uh, Carmen? Time for us to move on, too, d'you think?'

He hoped the wife he grieved over for so long could hear him. The Indians figured their relations could hear, so why not his?

He made his way up to the grave on the hill overlooking their valley. He could take her body with him to Omaha, of course, but Carmen belonged here and he would not change that.

Maybe he should have stuck it out here – however, he could always visit and he would. But, dammit, the decisions in life were never easy.

The publishers hope that this book has given you enjoyable reading. Large Print Books are especially designed to be as easy to see and hold as possible. If you wish a complete list of our books please ask at your local library or write directly to:

Dales Large Print Books
Magna House, Long Preston,
Skipton, North Yorkshire.
BD23 4ND